THE COLOUR OF HIS HAIR

AUTHOR'S NOTE

'Stories never really end,' Mary Norton said in *The Borrowers Aloft*. 'They can go on and on and on – and on: it is just that at some point or another the teller ceases to tell them.' *The Colour of His Hair* is not the last book I shall write, but it is the last novel. Il faut cultiver notre jardin.

THE COLOUR OF HIS HAIR

David Rees

THIRD HOUSE (PUBLISHERS)

First published in 1989 by Third House (Publishers)
69, Regent Street, Exeter, EX2 9EG, England

Copyright © David Rees 1989

ISBN 1 870188 10 1

Typeset by Rapid Communications Ltd, London WC1X 9NW
Printed by Billing & Sons, Ltd, Worcester

Distributed in the United Kingdom and in Western Europe by
Turnaround Distribution Co-op Ltd, 27, Horsell Road, London, N5 1XL

Distributed in the United States of America by Inland Book Company,
254, Bradley Street, East Haven, Connecticut, 06512, U.S.A.
and
Bookpeople, 2929, Fifth Street, Berkeley, California, 94710, U.S.A.

Distributed in Australia by Wild & Woolley Pty Ltd,
16, Darghan Street, Glebe, New South Wales 2007, Australia

Distributed in New Zealand by Benton Ross (Publishers) Ltd,
Unit 2, 46, Parkway Drive, Glenfield, Auckland 9, New Zealand

Cover photograph: Ian David Baker

There lives within the very flame of love
A kind of wick or snuff that will abate it
— Shakespeare, *Hamlet*

For Jim Palmer

PART ONE
1976

ONE

'Hey, this is a bit unusual, isn't it?'

My brother Donald grinned. 'I just thought I needed the exercise,' he said. There was a hint of embarrassment in his face.

I was about to take our dog, Sally, for a walk: Donald had invited himself to come along too. He hadn't done this for years, not since he was eleven or twelve. Once upon a time he had liked to think Sally was his dog, but when he became a teenager he lost interest. He had other concerns: football, and his gang of friends. It wasn't only the dog he lost interest in; he didn't have much time now for me. Though I could be wrong about that: it could be my fault, busy with 'O' levels, then 'A' levels and my boyfriend, Brian; I could be the one responsible for the distance. Donald was seventeen, a year younger than me; tall, lanky, attractive: dark hair, and green eyes that could look at you very disconcertingly if he suspected you weren't telling the truth. In the mornings now, before he went to school, he shaved. He was growing up.

It was a wintry February day, with the kind of chill that seems to get to your bones. Fog shrouded the tops of the trees in the park; damp dripped from twigs. Wallflowers and forget-me-nots the Council had planted were still withered from recent frosts, but one brave specimen, some sort of daisy, was in full bloom: a bunch of white petals. We chased the dog to keep warm, threw sticks for her. Donald had brought a football with him, and we belted it back and forth to each other; just like old times when we were both young kids. The dog barked her head

9

off; we shouted, screamed, laughed, ran everywhere, as if we really *were* young kids. What created this happy mood I don't know, but I liked it.

It didn't last long, however. Donald, having retrieved the football from a clump of forsythia bushes where I'd kicked it, put it under his arm and said, 'Helen, I have to talk to you.'

'What about?'

'I'm in love.'

'Oh?' I stared at him. I had never thought of Donald being in love before, but, well, it would obviously happen sooner or later; as I said, he was growing up. 'Who is she?' I asked.

'It isn't a she.' I must have looked rather blank, for he added, loudly and slowly, as if I was an idiot, 'He is a boy. Mark Sewell.'

Mark Sewell was in my 'A' level English group. He was eighteen – born the week before me – blond, blue-eyed, and very handsome. He could have been a brilliant games player if he had ever bothered, and he was the last person on earth you would imagine to be a pouf, even though – now I came to think of it – he never seemed to have girlfriends. Then my brother, the school's first eleven centre forward, was also the last person on earth you would imagine. . .

It began to dawn on me what Donald was saying. I was shocked. Stunned. Then I said to myself: I just don't believe it. 'Is this some kind of joke?' I asked.

'No, Helen. It isn't.' He sat down on a nearby bench, hands in pockets, legs crossed; a defiant but somehow scared look on his face. 'I've never been more serious in my life,' he said. We gazed at each other in silence for some moments. Our breath steamed. The dog, annoyed that her stick-chasing fun had stopped, came leaping over to us, her eyes quizzical; she growled, then decided it wasn't worth the effort and lay on the path, sighing heavily.

'I'm sorry for you,' I said.

'I'm not sorry for myself,' he answered. 'So why should you be?'

10

'You had better explain it all.' I sat down beside him. 'In words of one syllable. It isn't a subject in which I'm well versed.'

'I'm . . . oh, I don't know that I can explain anything! Look . . . I love him. Just as you do Brian, or at least as I imagine you do Brian. . .'

'What does Mark think about it?'

'He loves me too. That's why I said I'm not sorry for myself . . . and that you shouldn't be.'

I whistled in surprise. It accounted for the lack of girlfriends, but I was still . . . shaken rigid. Plenty of girls I knew would be disappointed if they heard this! Not that they would. Donald was sure to make me swear I'd keep this information to myself. 'How did it happen?' I asked. 'I mean . . . *why*? And how? How do you know? And why *you*? And . . . what do you do together?'

'Helen! Really! Have I ever asked what you do with Brian?'

I hadn't meant that. I'd meant what interests did they share; did they listen to symphonies on Radio Three or go to cricket matches. I thought: I don't know either of these people – my own brother, and a boy I've been in the same class with for seven years. Every certainty I'd felt about anything was suddenly reduced to no more than an assumption. 'Why are you telling me all this?' I asked.

'Because . . . because nobody else knows. You have to talk to someone about the most significant thing that has ever happened to you! I've thought, sometimes, it's O.K. for Helen! When Joanna or Pat says, "Did you and Bri have a good time last night?" you can *tell* them! You can compare notes about your boyfriends, and so on. I could hardly say to Gary or Jake or Andy or any of the other kids in the football team that when Mark was kissing me last night he said, "I love you." You can well imagine what they'd think! Helen . . . are you shocked?'

My brain was racing. For a few minutes I looked at my breath rise in the raw February air, then I said, 'Am I shocked? Yes. Not by the fact. I mean, it doesn't matter to me whether it's a boy or a girl . . . so long as the people

11

concerned are happy. But shocked – in the sense of being amazed – that it's *you*. Why you?'

'Perhaps you're asking yourself will I be like this all my life,' Donald said. 'Grow up never to get married, not to have children.'

I was silent again, thinking. 'I'm sorry you have to lead such a hidden existence,' I said.

'Yes. I am too. I can't bring him home and say, "Mum . . . Dad . . . I want you to meet my boyfriend." And that's a shame, Helen. Depressing. Disheartening.'

'Mum would freak out!'

'Yes.'

'As for Dad. . .'

'He'd probably want to have me psychoanalysed. Or locked up.'

'I don't think locked up,' I said. 'But . . . to put it mildly . . . he wouldn't be pleased. Probably go back on the bottle.' Dad, when we were younger, had been an alcoholic. It was always touch and go as to whether he'd start drinking again. 'Isn't it illegal, if you . . . do anything? Aren't you under age, both of you?'

'I could be prosecuted. Fined. Even put into care. As for you and Brian, you're heterosexual and over sixteen, so it's O.K. Doesn't seem right, does it! Well, I don't reckon it's right.'

'How long have you been . . . like this?'

'Years! Ever since I first knew about sex. When I was . . . twelve.' I must have looked even more astonished, for he said, 'I'm not unique! There are others; Mark knows a few. Ted Viner, maybe.'

I laughed. 'That's just a story!'

'How can you be certain of that?'

'I can't.' Ted Viner taught us English. He was thirty-eight years old and single, and because he had never got married the kids at school often joked that he must be queer. He was a good teacher. He drove his pupils hard; it was impossible to get away with scrimped, badly done work in his lessons, and his enthusiasm for his subject was infectious: it was Ted who had made me feel I'd like to study English literature at a university. I hadn't ever

12

stopped to consider, seriously, why he was unmarried, but I did now. Perhaps the stories were true.

'Most of the kids think Ted is O.K.,' Donald said. 'He's a nice enough geezer, doesn't shout and yell all the time. I like English, just as you do . . . Mark says Ted knows about him and me, that he's guessed.'

At this point the dog decided she had had enough of lying down on a path, and that we had had enough of sitting on a bench. She began to bark so much we could scarcely hear ourselves speak. Donald stood up and threw a stick for her. 'Don't repeat this conversation to anyone,' he said. 'Not even to Brian. On second thoughts, especially not to Brian.'

'Why especially not?'

'He might get very funny with Mark.'

'I shouldn't think so for a minute! But of course I'll keep your secret.'

I must have looked reluctant, however, for Donald said, 'Well . . . if you have to tell him, then you have to . . . but I'd prefer you didn't.'

We went home. I was surprised by how ordinary everything seemed, how exactly the same as when we had walked in this direction an hour previously; after Donald's earth-shattering confessions it should all, I felt, look different. The fog in the trees that made branches wraith-like and faint, the frost-bitten flowers, the damp; then, outside the park, the familiar bits of our West Croydon scenery – the shop with the peculiar name, *Tammy's Tropicals* (source of many a joke, that), the gap in a terrace where two men for over a year had been trying to build a house, the wall on which somebody had mis-spelled in spray paint: VOTE CONSERERIVE. And my brother, I said to myself, my little brother Donny, whom I remember at the age of five howling because he'd cut his leg, who looked quite sweet as a seven-year-old in shorts, who even now lived, I'd imagined, only for Wednesdays and Saturdays when he could kick footballs, was having an affair with someone of his own sex! *Mark!* Did they plan a future together, as Brian and I sometimes did? Talk of kitchens and curtains and wedding rings as

13

I did with my friend Joanna? It was weird, fantastic, grotesque!

I longed to tell Brian. He might be able to give it shape and sense. But I couldn't tell Brian; I'd promised Donald not to.

'Helen, what is the matter?' Ted Viner asked.

'Nothing, sir.' I blushed, and stared hard at my copy of *The Nun's Priest's Tale*.

'You haven't been paying attention the whole morning!'

It was true; I hadn't. I'd been watching Mark across the gangway from me when he was following the Chaucer in his text-book or looking out of the window, or twiddling with a strand of his long fair hair or doodling on a bit of paper; and I listened intently when Ted asked him to translate. Donald hadn't said so, but he'd implied it: they'd had sex. This guy was mucking about with my kid brother! That was one way of putting it, and it sounded just as improbable as saying 'Mark and Donald are lovers.' What was he like, this Mark, this boy I'd known since he was a pale-skinned, pale-haired eleven-year-old, now eighteen and nearly a man? What did he think, feel, believe in? What sort of parents did he have? Did Donald find his interests and hobbies absorbing?

Alison Reilly hadn't done her homework properly, and Ted was making her feel as withered as the flowers I'd seen yesterday in the park. Poor Alison! Wayne Stephens's fault: he took up too much of her time. As Ted's attention was so involved with Alison, Mark thought it an opportune moment to write me a surreptitious letter. It landed on my desk as poor Alison came to the brink of tears. Block capitals: WILL YOU STOP STARING AT ME? IT'S GETTING ON MY NERVES. Underneath this message was a skull and crossbones.

I screwed it up and hurled it at the wastepaper basket, breathed heavily, and began to concentrate on Chaucer's story of the hen and the cockerel.

I admired Donald. His behaviour, for a boy of seventeen who was attracted to his own sex, was, I guess, unusual;

14

he had not freaked out, or refused to admit to it because Gary and Jake and Andy might discover what he was, or pretended to himself that it could be a phase he'd shrug off like an illness in a few weeks' time.

'Mark was a great help,' he said, when I asked him about this. 'I think . . . if I hadn't met him, I'd be in a bit of a mess right now.'

'Does he like girls? I mean as friends.' I was wondering about the note he had written to me.

'Sure he does. Why not?'

I was learning too. From my young brother, of all people! If I'd thought at all about homosexuality, I'd said to myself girls like that gave me the creeps because they might fancy me and I couldn't cope with it; and as for the boys, well, it was a pity: it was so many fewer boys for the girls to get interested in. I hadn't ever considered the problems of being gay, the difficulty of telling oneself it was just as good and valid as it was to be attracted to the opposite sex. 'Does Mark know other gay people?' I asked.

'I thought I said that. Yes. Some. He took me to a pub . . . I didn't like it. I don't think I'm ready, I suppose. I mean, I feel a bit bothered going into a pub anyway because I'm only seventeen; what if the landlord insists on knowing how old I am and chucks me out? It hasn't ever happened, but that, and a crowd of men who . . . looking at me . . . I mean, I said to myself, what do they want from me?'

'Did they want anything?'

'I don't know. I just felt uneasy, so I clung to Mark.' He laughed. 'That was the good bit! A place with other people where we could hold hands and it didn't matter. It was nice!'

Mum called up from the kitchen: 'Dinner's on the table!' It was Sunday lunch-time, and we were in Donald's bedroom, the attic of the house. I was always rather jealous of Donald having the attic; it had two windows, sloping ceilings, and better views than I had from my ordinary old bedroom. His ownership of the attic had turned it into a typical teenage boy's room – pictures of

15

rock stars and sportsmen on the walls, a mobile made of racing bikes, and discarded games kit littering the floor – Mum was always complaining about this. I had to move a tennis racket, a pair of sneakers and two muddy shirts before I could sit down that morning. But there were also signs of interests more typically Donald than just an average teenage boy, though nothing anyone would consider particularly odd these days: CND posters, a cartoon of ex-President Nixon that he was using as a dart-board, a placard that announced: I AM A BORN-AGAIN ATHEIST. But there *was* something odd, I realised. No pin-ups – no scantily dressed girls. And placed among the football photos so discreetly that Mum wouldn't even see it when she was doing the dusting was someone I recognized. Mark.

Roast lamb and mint sauce, roast potatoes, sprouts and carrots. Dad carving the joint. A scene so normal, so unchanging throughout the eighteen years of my life that I blinked, astonished. Donald had so upset my belief in the normal that I didn't think Dad, cutting a slice of lamb and saying to me, 'Enough, Helen? Plenty more here if you want it,' was quite real.

'Is it cooked through?' Mum asked. 'I'm always worried with lamb that I'll undercook it.'

'It's nice and juicy,' Dad answered. 'Just how it ought to be. How many spuds, Donald?'

'Four.'

'Four *please*.'

We ate for a while in silence, then Mum said, 'Shame about this fog. I feel like going out for a drive this afternoon. However . . . I could pop over to Hilda's. We're making lampshades and we're not getting on with them quickly enough.'

'Because you two spend all your time gossiping over cups of tea,' Dad said. He looked out of the window. 'We could go out for a drive if you want to. Just because it's foggy here doesn't mean it's foggy everywhere.'

'No need to waste the petrol if it *is* foggy everywhere. Says in today's paper the price is going up. More sprouts, anyone?' Before we could answer, she began to dish them

16

onto our plates. 'They'll only be put in the bin if they're not eaten; when you cook them up again they always turn soggy.'

'Foggy soggy,' Donald said. 'I didn't know you talked in rhyme, Mum.' A grin hovered at the corners of his mouth, and his eyes signalled that he was trying to repress a great deal of laughter. The effect on me was catastrophic – a fit of hysterical giggles. I couldn't stop. It was the contrast between our recent conversations and those of Mum and Dad: Donald shook his head slightly, and frowned, as if to say, 'Don't let them think something strange is going on!'

'Helen!' Mum said, crossly. 'It isn't in the least bit funny!'

'Teenagers!' Dad snorted. 'More like little children. Grow up, the pair of you! Helen! Pull yourself together!'

TWO

The following weekend I did something I bitterly regretted. I told Brian.

He brought the subject up, but that didn't mean I had to say anything; I could have fended him off. He's doing 'A' level Chemistry, Maths and Physics, and he has that condescending air all the science students at our school have towards the arts students – arts are O.K. for girls, but for boys English and so on is a bit cissy. Science, they seem to think, is where the *real* work of the world is done, and women don't have a role in that: unimportant old English is fine for us because we'll sooner or later get married, have kids, and become housewives. Needless to say I object strongly to such attitudes, which caused the biggest row Brian and I ever had: the result was Brian doesn't talk like that any more, though I guess he still thinks that way.

We've been going out for nearly three years. He's very good-looking, sane, mature – and thoughtful. Except for the arts/science thing he doesn't usually give me the impression that he considers girls have inferior brains, or are merely useful for sex, or exist just to cook meals and wash socks. He's gentle. I grew to love him. But recently I'd been asking myself if love wasn't now growing a bit thin; I was finding Brian predictable. Perhaps even boring. That may account for my annoyance with his response when I told him – I hadn't reckoned on his lack of understanding when it came to the subject of homosexuality. We were on our way home from a disco; Saturday night – it should have been a pleasant, enjoyable evening out, the two of us with my friend Pat and her

18

boyfriend Keith. I used to love dancing with Brian: we were a good pair; music, rhythm, us – it made a whole. But this, also, was becoming predictable. I began to define the problem more clearly that evening. It was something which revealed itself when Brian was with male friends, not on occasions when he and I were alone: the stupid stories they swopped, the swilling down of pints of beer, the childish . . . competition: yes, that's the right word . . . that seems to go on between boys when they get together. The function of their girlfriends changes then. We cease to be the one person of importance; it's as if we're being regarded as prizes to show off to all and sundry. My bird's got bigger tits than your bird. Nobody says that of course, at least not in front of us, but that kind of suggestion is floating in the air.

Was it at this point I came to a subconscious decision to finish with him? I don't know. But I do remember thinking, as he and Keith tried to outshine each other in their knowledge of what went on inside the engine of a Triumph Herald, that I was bored, and that Brian's face was not always so attractive: it sometimes glistened, sweatily, where he shaved. My thoughts turned to Donald. How different this scene would be for him! No girlfriends, no showing off to his mates. Perhaps he wouldn't ever come to a disco such as this, or only very occasionally. But . . . what was all this like transferred to a gay context? I knew they had their own discos. And similar jealousies, I imagine. They wouldn't be able to walk home arm in arm, however, or hold hands on the bus, or kiss in the street. Donald had already said that; the ordinary little pleasures which we took for granted – he might never have them.

Brian and Keith had left car engines; it was Irish jokes now. 'Do you know what Irish foreplay is?' Keith asked.

'No.'

'Brace yourself, Bridget.'

A deal of laughter at this from both of them; Pat and I just raised our eyebrows. 'Do you know the definition of an Irish pervert?' Brian asked.

'Yes,' Keith said. 'A man who wants women more than he wants Guinness.'

The mention of the word 'pervert', I suppose, led to the next joke. 'Do you know what happened when Oscar Wilde fell into the sea?'

'No.'

'He came up clinging to the bottom of a buoy.' Keith looked blank, so Brian explained: 'B-O-Y. B-U-O-Y. It's a pun, thick-head.'

Even as recently as last week I would have taken no notice, but tonight I felt uncomfortable. I began to think how much the Irish, the gays – any minority – would detest this sort of fooling. I said, 'Why don't you stop that? You could be talking about your closest friend.' Perhaps there was something edgy in my voice, because Brian, on the way home, asked me why I'd said it; was there a particular reason? No, I answered, but he didn't look convinced.

'I wouldn't be happy if I found out my closest friend was gay,' he said.

'Why not?'

'I guess . . . I'd be frightened he'd be after me.'

We had just got off the bus and were walking up my road; the night was cold and I was looking forward to being indoors, to making Brian a cup of coffee and sitting with him on the sofa in front of the fire. His arms round me, reassuring me that he wasn't insensitive and dull. 'I think that's a *dreadful* thing to say!' I exploded. (I'd forgotten that I'd thought the same myself, about gay girls.)

'Why?' He was puzzled.

'Because you flatter yourself it's your body he'd want! Wouldn't he more likely be after – if that's the right word – someone who's also gay?'

'Helen . . . what *is* going on?'

'Nothing.' I opened my handbag, and searched for my keys.

'I want to know what it's about,' Brian persisted.

If you have to tell him, then you have to, Donald had said. He'd also said 'I'd prefer you didn't.'

Mum and Dad were still up, watching a foreign film on TV. 'I don't understand a word of it,' Dad said, 'but your mother seems to think it's all very marvellous.'

'Where's Donald?'

'Staying overnight at a friend's.'

'Who?'

'Mark . . . uh . . . I can't remember his surname.'

'Coming into the kitchen, Brian?' He followed me out of the room, thinking, I guess, that I'd make coffee, but I said, 'Let's go upstairs. I want to show you something.' I took him to the attic and pointed at the photograph on the wall.

'It's Mark Sewell! What's he doing here?'

He looked astonished when I told him, then uneasy, and, finally, very disapproving. 'I can't take this,' he said. 'It's creepy!'

'What do you mean, creepy?'

'It's unnatural. Wrong! Donald! The first eleven centre forward! How can it be? It's not possible! I never did like Mark very much. Something . . . phoney about him. Now he's going round corrupting your brother.'

'I don't think you've listened to a word I've said, Brian! I did not say Donald has been corrupted. He seems a more than willing partner.'

'Jesus! What's got into the pair of them?'

'Nothing's got into them,' I said. 'It's how they are.'

'Well . . . I don't want anything to do with it.'

'Nobody's asked you to.'

'Helen . . . why are you telling me all this?'

I'd put the same question to Donald. You have to talk to someone about the most significant thing that has ever happened to you, he'd said, and though it wasn't the most significant thing that had ever happened to *me*, it had . . . changed me. Changed my perception of my brother, for instance. Of the minority he belonged to. 'Because it's on my mind,' I said to Brian. 'It disturbs me – for Donald's sake, I mean. I'm not disturbed by the fact of it, as you seem to be. It's things like . . . what sort of an existence does he have in the future? Does he go on pretending to his mates that he isn't? Or find a new lot of friends – gay ones? What if Mum and Dad discover? And because the jokes you and Keith make aren't amusing any longer.'

21

'I agree the jokes aren't brilliant. But they don't hurt anyone. And . . . when you say what if your Mum and Dad discover, I take it you think it would be bad if they did. I think they *should* know. In order to get Donald straightened out.'

I stared at him, hardly believing what I'd heard. It seemed so . . . pig ignorant. 'How do you suggest we straighten Donald out?' I said, trying to sound as sarcastic as possible.

'I don't know . . . doctors . . . psychiatrists?'

'I didn't realise till now that you were such an absolute moron. A complete idiot.'

He said, 'I'm going downstairs to watch the end of the film! I often think I get better conversations with your parents than I do with you.' He stumped out, bewildered and annoyed.

Not, however, as annoyed as I was. I went to my room, took off my clothes and got into bed. I didn't care very much if Brian felt awkward saying to Mum and Dad that he didn't know where I'd gone; or, if they guessed I was in my room, that he might have to invent some reason for why I was there.

He phoned next day, but he wasn't puzzled or angry. 'Oh, I just assumed you were tired,' he said.

Donald and Mark were very discreet. You didn't notice them in each other's company at school, and they didn't walk there together. There were, of course, a number of places on the premises where they could be private; I knew that from my relationship with Brian. Donald, if he was seen with anybody, was with his football friends – Gary, Andy and Jake. Mark I'd always considered a loner; he'd never gone around in a gang. I found myself walking behind him one morning. He was aware it was me, for he stopped, waited for me to catch up, and said, 'Donald says he told you.' He smiled. 'I'm pleased . . . grateful . . . you took it so well.'

Something about this remark made me a bit uncomfortable. 'It's no big deal,' I said, staring intently at the house we happened to be passing. Then I looked up at him and said, 'You shouldn't have to be grateful! In ordinary circumstances gratitude wouldn't come into it.'

He laughed. 'That's perfectly true. But boy loving boy is extraordinary circumstances. Donald needed to talk to someone, perhaps . . . I'm not sure . . . to put himself and me back into the rest of his life. To stop thinking our time together occurs on a different planet. I'll be honest . . . I didn't really want him to tell you.'

'Why?'

'Because of Brian. I haven't anything against Brian, but there's this sixth sense, this intuition that warns me it might mean trouble.'

I hoped I wasn't blushing so crimson he'd guess at once that I'd already given his secret away. I concentrated on a nearby front garden – jasmine in bloom, a yellow patch of crocuses on the lawn – and tried to look serene. 'I don't know how much longer Brian and I will be together,' I mumbled.

'Oh?' As I said nothing further, Mark probably assumed I'd already revealed more than I wanted to; he changed the subject back to himself and Donald. 'I'm lucky,' he said. 'I've been able to talk to my parents.'

'To your *parents*!' The idea was inconceivable.

'Yes.' He was amused; the expression of astonishment on my face, I suppose. 'They've always been pretty liberal,' he said. 'Some adults *are*, Helen.' His father was a social worker and a Labour member of the Borough Council; my father was a scrap metal dealer and never bothered to vote; all politicians, he said, were liars. Maybe that led to liberal attitudes, and vice versa. 'I told them I was sure I was gay about six months ago. When Donald and I–'

'Six months ago! I'd thought . . . this all started a couple of weeks back!'

'Beginning of the autumn term. The first time we spoke was in the changing-room at school . . . I'd fancied him for months. Then next day I saw him in the park, the one where you walk your dog. I think we both knew by then. If we hadn't, I wouldn't have dared to say what I said next . . . I asked him to go out with me. We went to the zoo.'

23

'I remember! He told me he'd been to Regent's Park. Unexpectedly.'

'After that . . . I found I was madly in love with him. He came over to my house, and . . . he fell off a ladder, in the garden. I caught him as he slipped, and . . . for a few moments . . . I held him. He was wanting me to kiss him.'

'Did you?'

'Yes.' He laughed. The look on his face seemed to suggest a perfect love life, a perfect relationship. Unlike me and Brian. 'I think I envy you,' I said.

'You don't have to go that far! The difficulties are enormous, as you can surely imagine. But I'm glad my parents were so positive. I don't suppose I'll ever forget the evening I told them. We were having our supper at the time. Liver and kidneys. Casseroled. They said they'd rather I wasn't . . . gay, I mean . . . but so long as I was happy . . . and that Donald seemed a nice person.'

'Has he stayed overnight before?'

'Last weekend was the first time. Your mum and dad didn't suspect anything, did they?'

'No. Not at all. Did you . . . enjoy yourselves?'

'We certainly did!' Again, the broad smile and the happy laugh.

We had reached school. Hundreds of kids were milling in the playground, shouting and screaming. A moment from some morning last year came into my head; I'd looked out of a classroom window at kids yelling and chasing each other or playing football, two boys fighting, girls giggling, a boy and a girl in a deep serious conversation – and I'd been reminded of the old advertising jingle of *The News of the World*: all human life is here. Now I was walking into that playground with a boy who represented a bit of human life I'd never have thought, on that previous occasion, existed in our school. Such is growing up, I said to myself, as Mark and I made our way to Ted's room – English first lesson, so we wanted to leave our books there before we went to Assembly.

Ted was vigorously rubbing something off the blackboard, which was odd – a quirk of his teaching methods was that he never used the blackboard. I once asked him why. 'I can't bear to touch chalk,' he said. 'And the sound of its squeak sends shivers up my spine.' He peered at us over the top of his spectacles, then returned to his rubbing. There wasn't much left of whatever it was that had to be erased; a bleeding heart, I think, with an arrow and drops of blood. Perhaps some kid had got in there and scribbled 'Ted Viner loves Doris Hatchett' – Miss Hatchett taught Geography in the next-door classroom and was about as horrific as her name suggests – but, it occurred to me, considering all the jokes that were repeated about Ted's sexual inclinations, the other name could have been a man's. Or a boy in the school.

'You won't need it,' Ted said to Mark, who was taking his Chaucer out of his bag. 'We're doing a critical appreciation this morning.'

'But we did one yesterday!' I objected. 'Edwin Muir – *The Horses*.'

'Yes, well, you're doing another one today; I think you're all sadly out of practice. The more literature you read, the more mature your mind becomes. There are far too many people in this school whose minds need a bit of maturing.'

'What on earth's got into him?' I said to Mark, as we hurried downstairs to Assembly.

'Probably jumped out of bed the wrong side,' he answered. Something to do with whatever was scribbled on the blackboard was my opinion.

I left Mark when we reached the Hall, and pushed my way through to where Brian was standing. En route I passed Donald, who winked and grinned. 'You all right?' I said. My first words to him that day; he and I had such totally different bathroom and breakfast routines that we rarely met at home in the mornings.

'Helen,' he said, 'you are always asking me these days if I'm all right! I am *not* ill!'

'Pardon me for *breathing*!'

'I'm sorry. I'm not being grumpy. But, yes' – he laughed – 'I *am* all right!'

I had been, as it were, taking his mental and emotional temperature a bit too frequently; as if, I began to realise,

25

I thought in my subconscious that homosexuality was some sort of disease. Which was absurd, considering it was not Donald's and Mark's relationship but mine and Brian's that had caught a chill.

'I wish you wouldn't go around with that pouf,' Brian said.

'What are you talking about?'

'Mark Sewell.'

'I'll go around with whoever I choose to go around with,' I said, angrily. 'I'm not taking orders from anyone! Least of all you!'

'Helen . . . I'm sorry. I don't want us to quarrel.' I didn't answer. 'What are you doing this evening?'

'Working. Ted is in a bad mood; he'll give us some very long, very boring essay to write at home.'

'Come round to my house if you need a break.'

'I'll . . . think about it.'

'Helen . . . what's the matter?'

I looked him straight in the eye. 'I'm not sure that I like you as much as I did once upon a time.'

He was amazed. He opened his mouth to speak but could not, as the Headmaster arrived in the Hall at that moment. Assembly began.

THREE

The poem Ted inflicted on us was by A.E. Housman:

Oh who is that young sinner with the handcuffs on his
wrists?
And what has he been after that they groan and shake
their fists?
And wherefore is he wearing such a conscience-
stricken air?
Oh they're taking him to prison for the colour of
his hair.

'Tis a shame to human nature, such a head of hair
as his;
In the good old time 'twas hanging for the colour
that it is;
Though hanging isn't bad enough and flaying would
be fair
For the nameless and abominable colour of his hair.

Oh a deal of pains he's taken and a pretty price
he's paid
To hide his poll or dye it of a mentionable shade;
But they've pulled the beggar's hat off for the world to
see and stare,
And they're taking him to justice for the colour of
his hair.

Now 'tis oakum for his fingers and the treadmill for
his feet,
And the quarry-gang on Portland in the cold and in
the heat,

And between his spells of labour in the time he has to
spare
He can curse the God that made him for the colour of
his hair.

Ted's stratagem never altered: he would invite us to
make comments, and wait in silence until the comments
came. This could be extremely disconcerting if nobody
had anything to say because Ted refused to give in and
do the work for us; he just sat there. The class couldn't
put up with this for too long – thus illustrating, I suppose,
the law about Nature detesting a vacuum – and someone
would eventually be driven to open his or her mouth. Ted
wouldn't answer. He'd just nod, negatively or positively,
or say 'Uh-huh' or 'Mm-mm' and wait for the next
comment. This usually went on for about half an hour
– it could be slow torture – then he'd make an analysis
of the poem, often with rude remarks for those students
who had contributed nothing. As a teaching method, it
was pretty effective.

Sometimes we would imitate his uh-huhs and mm-mms
out loud, which he didn't mind; he'd just grin. He
had all sorts of mannerisms – touching his lips with
his forefinger, blowing his nose when he didn't need
to, scratching the back of his neck, raising his thick
bushy eyebrows until they almost disappeared. We often
wondered how he managed to keep order; it would be
easy, we felt, to reduce his lessons to chaos if we wanted
to. But it never happened.

His first sentence of the day was in answer to the girl
sitting next to me, my friend Joanna, who wanted to know
what 'poll' meant. 'Look it up in the dictionary,' he said,
'and read it out to the class.'

She did so. ' "The head, or the hair of the head," ' she
announced. 'Uh-huh. I might as well look up oakum too
while I'm at it. Mm-mm . . . here it is: "old tarred ropes
untwisted and teased out for caulking the seams of ships."
Was that prisoners' work in the old days?'

Ted nodded.

A picture came into my mind of slaves in Roman galleys, straining at the oars. Then I thought of Donald, who had recently taken up rowing for the school's somewhat incompetent first eight.

'Is Portland the Isle of Portland in Dorset?' Peter Thomas asked. 'Is there a prison there?'

'Uh-huh,' Ted murmured.

'I don't like this poem,' said Mark. 'It just isn't very good. It's doggerel. No word or phrase in it that's outstanding.' There was a mutter of agreement from the whole class, and Ted's eyebrows vanished. 'It makes me feel uncomfortable,' Mark went on. Ted looked at him for a moment, then nodded in approval.

'Why does he say "beggar"?' Kelvin Burnett asked. 'Why doesn't he say what he obviously means – bugger?' Everyone laughed at this, and Ted vigorously blew his nose.

'You can't put things like that in print,' Alison objected.

'Why not?'

'It isn't nice.'

Several people protested that it was merely a word, and that if you wanted to say it in print, then you should be allowed. 'Get back to the poem,' Ted said.

'Perhaps he is a bugger,' said Jason Smith, a small, impish boy with mischievous, dark eyes, one of the more thoughtful members of the class. 'Perhaps that's why he's going to prison.'

We all looked at Ted for confirmation of this, but his face was absolutely blank for a moment. Then he stared at Jason, rather intently, as if he was asking himself a question.

'Buggery isn't a crime,' Tom Harding said. 'Is it?' He was the dunce of our group, the one we all considered most likely to fail the exam.

'Maybe it was when the poem was written,' Jason said.

I glanced at Mark. His jaw was set, his face as blank as Ted's.

'He's going to prison for the colour of his hair,' Tom said. 'Which doesn't make sense. It's rather a silly poem. Why should anybody be chucked in the nick because of their hair? It doesn't even say *what* colour it is!'

'Green,' Mark said. 'Like you.' I looked at him again, in surprise this time; he sounded angry.

'It's nameless and abominable, his hair,' Joanna said. 'Verse two, line four.'

'It's silly,' Tom repeated. 'He's writing it just for the sake of writing it. He's letting himself get carried away. Words, words, words.' He pushed the poem across his desk, and leaned back in his seat, hands behind his head.

Ted wriggled as if a bug had got inside his shirt, and he scratched the back of his neck. Then he stared at Jason again.

The discussion continued for some time; nobody thought the poem particularly memorable – the language was ordinary, and the rhythm too diddly-dee to suit the subject matter. Tom was wrong, Jason said, about why the man was being jailed; 'the colour of his hair' was a metaphor. 'The poet could have written,' Jason said, ' "But they've pulled the beggar's hat off for the world to see and *grin*, And they're taking him to justice for the colour of his *skin*." '

'Why didn't he?' Tom asked. 'Tell us that.'

Jason thought for a moment, then said, 'I don't know.'

'Not bad, not bad at all,' Ted said. 'You're not quite such a dreary crowd of imbeciles as I'd begun to imagine. In fact you've left very little for me to say. It certainly isn't a great poem, maybe not even a good poem. But it puts its point forcefully. Sarcastically. I wouldn't criticise the diddly-dee rhythm – dreadful word, diddly-dee! Where did you drag it up from, Helen? The rhythm is that of a song, the kind of song that used to be written for occasions like public hangings. Perhaps it's meant to reflect the shallow, vindictive nature of the people singing the song, the bystanders watching him go to prison, who think being flayed alive is the correct punishment for a person with that hair colour. Now Jason's point about hair colour being a metaphor: he's quite right, of course, and to say the poet could mean skin colour is a perfectly reasonable interpretation. Plenty of men and women the world over are in prison because of the colour of their skin. Nelson Mandela, for example, and hundreds of other blacks in South Africa. But Tom asked why Housman *didn't* say skin colour, which is just as reasonable as Jason's comment. The answer is, perhaps, that he didn't want to nail the supposed crime to any one social injustice in particular. So the poem refers to more than skin colour – people are incarcerated for their religious beliefs, for their political affiliations, and so on. I said *perhaps* that's the answer. I think, myself, that Housman *is* referring to one particular social injustice. The nameless and abominable colour of his hair, as Joanna rightly said – "the love that dares not speak its name." Have you any thoughts on what that could be?'

No one had any idea.

'I'm not surprised you can't guess,' Ted went on, 'though Jason came pretty near it. There are social injustices that stay hidden. You can see a black, can't you? But what colour is a homosexual?'

That word – I couldn't recall a teacher ever using it before in a class I was in – produced an immediate tension. Would any other word have done so? I doubt it. The strain, however, collapsed as soon as Tom answered Ted's question: 'They're effeminate,' he said. People grinned and laughed. 'Well, they are,' he mumbled.

'Really, Tom! You've been watching too many stereotypes on second-rate television programmes! But to return to the poem – it's about attitudes to homosexuality. One in ten people is gay or partly gay, which means there's at least one in this room, and I'm talking of *you* lot. I'm not including myself – interpret that how you will.' He smiled, which was daring of him, I thought. 'Nowadays they don't have to pick oakum for years just because of their sexual behaviour. Nevertheless, they're often persecuted. Subtly persecuted. Discriminated against. Why am I telling you all this? Because it goes on in this school. Right now. When I came in here this morning, there was something written on the blackboard. It isn't the first time it's happened this week, though not previously in this room. Messages have been scribbled on various blackboards throughout the school, referring, all of them, to the same two people. I want it stopped. I want *you* to

31

see that it's stopped. My sixth-form English set – you're some of the most intelligent and decent kids in this jungle: if anyone can do it, you can.' The bell rang for the end of the lesson. 'O.K.,' Ted said. 'Clear off and think about what I've been saying.'

Mark and I were the last to leave. When all the others had gone, he said, 'I suppose one of the names was mine.'

Ted was fiddling with some papers, rather deliberately. Then he blew some non-existent dust off the top of a pile of books. 'Why should you imagine that?' he said, eventually.

'Was it? Or wasn't it?'

Ted looked at him, then at me, then at Mark again. 'The second name was Helen's brother,' he said.

'Can we talk to you?'

There was another long pause before Ted spoke. 'Not now. I have a class.'

I left the room hurriedly. I couldn't face being alone with Mark; what was happening, I was sure, was my fault because I'd told Brian. Not that Brian, despite what he had said about his feelings on the subject, would have gone around the school scribbling on blackboards; he wasn't so juvenile – but who had he told? And who had that boy – or girl – told?

'Keith. That's all. Helen, I didn't want this –'

'No, I don't suppose you did. But one person tells one other, strictly in confidence – naturally! – then that person tells his friend, strictly in confidence too, then *that* person. . . It goes on like a game of Chinese Whispers. In less than a week it's all public knowledge.'

'You're a fine one to talk!' Brian said. '*You* started it, didn't you!'

'You're absolutely right. I'm guiltier than anyone else. I feel . . . awful.'

He put his arm round me. I wanted to shrug it off, but I didn't. I needed him – someone, anyone – at that moment. I wasn't very pleased with myself. 'I don't know who's doing it,' he said. '*I'm* not. And I'm sure Keith isn't.

32

We're far too old for stupid things like that! It's the work of . . . second years, third years. . .'

'Or someone who has a grudge. An idiot who thinks hanging isn't bad enough and flaying would be fair.'

'What?'

'Oh . . . a poem we were doing with Ted, first period. Brian . . . it's got to be stopped!'

'I don't see how you're going to do that.'

'Find out who's been told,' I said.

'What was actually written on Ted's board?'

'He didn't say, apart from the names. I saw him rubbing it out, but all I noticed was a bleeding heart.'

We were in a corner of the sixth-form common room, which was in the newest wing of the school, built last summer: our year was the first sixth form to occupy it. I had felt proud of that once upon a time, but not now; it had quickly become a shambles. Too many of us didn't know how to treat it properly. The furniture was coffee-stained; there were cigarette butts ground into the floor; the kettle didn't work because someone had used it as a football, and the sink had no taps – they had been unscrewed and stolen. A jungle, Ted had called the school. Not the right choice of word: the animals in a jungle look after their environment.

'I don't know what to do,' Brian said.

'You could be friendly to Mark.'

'I'm not unfriendly. Listen . . . are you busy tonight? Why don't you come round? My parents are going to a film . . . we can have the place to ourselves. I don't seem to have seen you recently.'

'You saw me yesterday.'

'I mean outside school.'

Perhaps I should try and patch things up with Brian, I thought. I needed a sympathetic ear, and it was absurd to make an enemy of him. 'O.K.,' I said.

It was similar to other evenings I'd spent alone with Brian, but it didn't work, not this time. Because, as I'd already said to him, I wasn't sure I liked him as much as I did once, and you can't respond physically or emotionally to a boy you don't like. Well . . . I can't.

I untangled myself from his arms, then went to the door; I had to go to the loo. 'I . . . think . . . we ought to see a bit less of each other for a while,' I said, as gently as I could. 'Until this Donald/Mark fuss has blown over, maybe. It's bothering me too much.'

He looked furious. 'I'm not having my love-life wrecked by some bloody poufter!' he shouted.

I felt sad, miserable, small. 'Then it's finished, Brian.'

'I'll kill him!'

'We behave absolutely normally,' Mark said. 'As if nothing has happened. We go through that playground just as we always do.' The three of us, for the first time, were walking to school together; it didn't matter, Mark and Donald had decided, if people saw them now: the nature of the relationship was known – yesterday Five B had seen the names and the drawings on Doris Hatchett's board. We were in a glum, serious mood, Donald especially. He had not panicked when he found out what had occurred, but he was more than worried: scared.

'I didn't sleep very well,' he said to me as we left the house. 'I don't know . . . I don't want to lose my friends. Their esteem . . . they're not so important since I met Mark, but even so . . . I was awake for hours imagining jeers and sneers, being sent to Coventry. Even physical violence.'

We need not have worried. There were no odd looks from anyone, no sniggers, no whispers. Gary called out to Donald: 'Did you see the game on TV last night?'

'Yes,' Donald answered. 'What a let-down!'

'Terrible, wasn't it!'

Tom waved cheerfully, and Joanna said, 'When did you two start going around together?' This question was addressed to me and Mark. It made all three of us giggle uncontrollably. 'Wasn't aware I had a role as the funny girl,' Joanna said. She looked puzzled.

'Hey Donald,' Andy said, 'that French translation we had to do for Ernie Pitt – what does *drapeau* mean?'

34

'*Le Drapeau Rouge*: the Red Flag.'

'Oh, God! I said it was a bit of old red cloth!'

'Do you really think,' said Jake, who was listening to this, 'that the Russians hang bits of old red cloth on the Kremlin walls?'

When we were on our own, I said, 'Seems strange. Everything's just as it normally is.'

'Good.' Mark heaved a sigh of relief. 'Perhaps we've all been over-reacting.' He and Donald looked at each other and smiled; it was the first time that day Donald's expression was other than tense and grim. He touched Mark's hand, briefly.

'See you at twelve thirty,' he said. 'Usual place?'

'Yes.'

Where was that, I wondered, but I didn't like to inquire. Mark and I turned to go up the stairs to Ted's room; Brian, coming down, saw us, scowled, and deliberately gazed out of a window until we had gone by.

'What's eating *him*?'

'We've split up.' I explained what had happened.

The worried frown returned to Mark's face. 'I don't want to be on bad terms with him,' he said. 'It bothers me.'

'I seem to have done just about every wrong thing I could have done.' I had told him and Donald, on the way to school, that I was the person responsible for their secret being known. Confession did not make me feel any better. In fact I felt so miserable I wasn't able to add, till now, that I'd ended with Brian.

Mark laughed, and gave me a hug. 'There are plenty more things I'm sure you can ruin,' he teased.

Ted was looking out for us. 'Come over here,' he said, and guided us to the window, away from the others in his room – Jason, Kelvin and Alison. 'You wanted to talk. But you didn't come back.'

'I . . . I thought I'd leave it,' Mark answered.

'I'm here if you want me.' Ted blew his nose. 'I have to tell you . . . the phantom blackboard graffiti specialist has struck again. *My* blackboard. That's twice this week.'

'Who the hell is it?'

'We'd all like to know *that*,' I said.

35

FOUR

Saturday night, disco night, but it was something completely new for me – I was going out with Donald and Mark on my first venture ever into a gay disco, and I was a little apprehensive. 'Don't worry,' Donald said. 'No one is going to rape you! No one's even going to chat you up!' He was much more cheerful now the school week was over, not that anything dramatic had happened in the past few days – the phantom blackboard graffiti specialist, as Ted had christened him, was lying low, and Five B had evidently dismissed the words in Miss Hatchett's room as a joke.

'I don't know that I like the idea of *not* being chatted up,' I said.

Donald laughed. 'You can't have it all ways, Helen.'

'Keep an eye on me. And rescue me if the girls come on too strong.'

'There's nothing to get bothered about! If you're not interested, they'll leave you alone. When I went last Saturday I was really nervous . . . I guess I was wondering how do I say no if somebody keeps trying to buy me a drink, or asks me to dance and I don't want to. Just like you say no to *anything* you don't want, I realised. Well . . . I was with Mark . . . so it was fine.'

'I thought you said you weren't ready for this sort of thing.'

'That was a couple of weeks ago!'

'Aren't you a bit young for such places?'

'Helen! You go to *your* discos! Why shouldn't I go to the ones that suit me? Anyway . . . this is only the second time I've ever been.'

'Mark, I suppose, is a hardened regular.'

'No. But he's been more often than I have.'

It was just like any other disco, I was relieved to find, except that boys for the most part were with boys, girls with girls. I hoped I wasn't calling attention to myself by being almost the only person there who danced with the opposite sex all evening – with either Donald or Mark, and occasionally with both of them at the same time. When I wasn't dancing, I stood at the edge of the floor watching them dance together. Once again I felt I had reason to envy them.

I began to notice differences, things I preferred to some of the scenes I'd witnessed in an ordinary disco. The men were better dressed on the whole and looked gentle; nobody spent the entire evening swallowing pints of beer and getting drunk. If a fight occurred, as it occasionally did in places I'd been to with Brian, it was more likely to be between the women, I thought, some of whom were distinctly unfeminine and aggressive-looking. But all remained peaceful.

I felt lonely on the way home: no arms round *me* tonight. No kisses. There weren't many kisses for Donald or Mark either, at least not after we left the disco. I said I could take myself back, but they wouldn't allow it; so I decided, if Mum and Dad had gone to bed, I'd go straight up to my room and let Donald and Mark have the privacy of downstairs. But they hadn't gone to bed: another foreign film – Channel Four was doing a Polish season – for Mum to think was marvellous and for Dad to grumble about.

'This one goes on till twenty to two!' Dad complained.

'That's in only half an hour's time,' Mum said, looking at the clock. 'You're all a bit late coming in, aren't you?'

Mark was introduced and I went out to the kitchen to make coffee. Mum followed me, as I knew she would. 'I'll tell you before you pop the question,' I said. 'We've split up. That's what you wanted to know, isn't it?'

She was surprised. 'How did you guess, Helen?'

I laughed. 'I can read you like a book, Mum.'

'Still . . . you've done all right for yourself, haven't you!'

'What do you mean?'

'Mark . . . is that his name? . . . He's *very* attractive.'

'Mark?' I tried my best not to look amazed, and just stopped myself saying, 'But he's *Donald's* boyfriend!' I hesitated a moment, then said, 'Of course . . . er . . . Mark.'

Mum said, 'Oh, you young people!' and went back to watch the film. As nobody else was in the kitchen I allowed myself, while I spooned Nescafé into the cups, to have a good laugh about her mistake. Predictable people, my parents. Which meant they expected everybody else to be predictable too.

The five of us saw the final struggles of a group of shipyard workers in Gdansk being shot at by the Polish army, then Mum leaned across to switch the television off, yawned, and said, 'I'm going to bed.' She nudged Dad.

He blinked, and muttered in reply, 'Oh . . . yes.'

At the door she said, 'Donald! Long past your bedtime.' Such was her unsubtle attempt to have Mark and me left on our own; when she had gone out with Dad and shut the door, the three of us found ourselves laughing quite helplessly for a few moments.

'Well, I won't play gooseberry either,' I said. 'Thank you for a very pleasant evening; I wouldn't object if we did it again some time. Donald . . . when Mark goes, *do* remember to put the lights out. You always forget, so if Mum finds them on in the morning, even she'll start to think there's something odd.'

When we got to school on Monday, the crowds parted for us as the sea for Israel. 'So it's true, then,' I heard a boy say: he was looking at Donald then at Mark. Somebody flapped a wrist, and sniggered. Another boy minced, hand grotesquely on hip. Wherever we walked people moved away from us. 'What on earth has happened?' Mark said. 'Have they done an item about us on TV? Profiled us in *The Sun*?' We did not have long to wait before we discovered the answer. There was an enormous crowd of kids staring at the far wall of the school building; this wall, which faced away from the road, had few windows,

just those at the end of corridors: so there was a great
stretch of brick which we soon knew had given the
phantom blackboard graffiti specialist considerable scope
for his abilities. I shan't repeat what was painted there,
nor describe the obscene drawings that accompanied the
comments. Sufficient to say that it told the world in no
uncertain terms that Donald and Mark were indulging in
a very sexual relationship.

Ted told us later that he had been standing next to the
Headmaster when he had first seen this – this atrocity,
he called it. The Headmaster had said, 'And do they? Is
it true?'

'It's none of our business,' Ted had replied. 'The truth
of it – or not – is hardly the point.'

'No indeed.' Ted was almost the only teacher the Head
listened to, it was rumoured. He had been at the school
ten years longer.

My feelings when I saw those vile messages and
revolting cartoons were anger, hatred and despair: there
was some person in the community who was utterly sick.
He must be ripped out, I said to myself; expelled, arrested,
sent to prison, shut up in some institution for the mentally
insane. If I got my hands on him, I wouldn't vouch for his
being in one piece for long. Or her. Could it be a girl? She
was so madly in love with Mark or Donald and therefore
so thwarted and frustrated she needed psychiatric treatment? Probably not.

Mark just stared; there was almost no visible change in
his expression. Donald, however, cried 'Oh, no! No!' and
beat his hands on his head. He staggered and nearly fell;
because of the shock, he said afterwards: his heart was
beginning to thump violently, his breath was coming in
spasms, and the muscles in his legs were so taut they
didn't seem to be capable of working properly. Mark,
in full view of two hundred or more kids and several
teachers, put his arms round Donald and held him tightly.
'Keep as calm as you can,' he said. 'Don't let them see it
could break you.'

At Assembly, the Headmaster said it was the worst
offence that had been committed in his entire six years at

39

the school, and that he would spare no effort in seeking out the culprit; but if the person or persons responsible owned up, their punishment would be the lighter. He knew, of course, that nobody would own up, but I suppose he had to say that. How on earth he thought he could find the culprit I couldn't imagine, unless the kid had paint on his clothes that matched the colour of the paint on the wall, or a trail of it led from the scene of the crime to the house where he lived.

Donald and Mark were summoned to the Head's office during first lesson. 'I've only one thing to say to you both,' the Headmaster said. 'Have you any idea who could have perpetrated this outrage? Is there anybody in the school – boy or girl – who harbours a grudge?'

'No sir,' Donald said.

Mark considered the question for a while. 'No one.'

The Headmaster looked at them, thoughtfully. 'Very well. Go back to your lessons.'

'That was good of him,' Mark said, when they were outside in the corridor.

'What?'

'Only *one* thing to say. He implied that he didn't want to know any specific details. About us. Such as, is it true? I'm not quite sure what to make of that.' He stared at Donald. 'God! You've been crying.'

'No.'

'You have.'

'All right. I have.' His face, Mark told me, was utterly forlorn: tear-stained, shocked, white.

'I . . . want to hold you. Touch you. Soothe away the hurt.'

Donald shook his head. 'We're standing outside the Headmaster's office!'

'I know.'

They went to their separate classrooms.

Solitude was the immediate problem. Nobody knew how to speak to them: some kids probably wanted to, but either did not have the words or were scared their friends would think them tarred with the same brush. Donald, who always sat next to Andy, found the desk beside

him, no matter what the lesson might be, was vacant.
Except in English: Ted ordered Andy to sit in the seat
he'd invariably occupied. Jake and Gary, too, kept out
of his way; whispered together, giggled. Then, when no
teachers were around, there were the taunts, not said to
his face, but undoubtedly meant for him to hear.

'Don't turn your back on him!'

'Does he wear a dress when he goes out with Mark
Sewell?'

'Keeps his lipstick in a handbag.'

'You can usually tell them by the way they walk.'

'I wouldn't bend down when *he's* in the room!'

'Does Sewell shove it up his bum?'

This last comment made Donald spring at the boy
who said it. 'I grabbed him by the throat,' he told me that
evening. 'I'd have throttled him if some other kids hadn't
intervened.'

Fortunately Ernie Pitt came round the corner at that
moment and sent everybody packing.

Mark was treated differently. Maybe because he was
older, or his actions that morning had shown him to be
the less vulnerable, there were no taunts. Or it could have
been that, unlike Donald, he had few connections with
the games players in the school. Apart from Joanna, who
spoke to him with a certain stiff politeness, and Jason,
who was no less friendly than usual, he was simply
ignored; in the sixth-form common room people suddenly
found a great interest in newspapers and textbooks when
he appeared. Not me. I tried to spend as much time as I
could with him, and with Donald too, but it wasn't easy:
Mark didn't have exactly the same lessons as me, and
Donald's and mine didn't coincide at all.

At midday I literally bumped into Brian; he was rushing
out of a door carrying half a dozen squash rackets, and
banged me on the head with them. 'Helen . . . I'm sorry,'
he said.

'It's all right. It didn't hurt.'

'I want to say this.' He spoke slowly, seeming to
choose his words with care. 'To do what Mark did . . .
in front of a whole crowd . . . to put his arms round a

41

boy! That took some guts. I think I've changed my mind about him.'

'In what way?' I asked.

'I think I'm beginning to admire him.'

'Are you the only one?'

'No. There are one or two others.'

'Then why don't you all *do* something?' My voice started to sound shrill.

He gestured, helplessly, with the squash rackets. 'What can we do? You know how it is. How people are.'

'Everyone's scared, Brian! Scared of their own silly shadows! Worried that they'll lose a little bit of their popularity! They all go around the whole time conforming! If they don't do precisely what everybody else does their mates won't want to be seen with them any more! Surely . . . what am I trying to say?' I found I was scratching the back of my neck, just as Ted did. Were these mannerisms of his, I wondered, attempts to coax himself into speech? 'I want to grow up to be *me*, whatever that "me" is. *Not* to have blue curtains in my bedroom just because Joanna does. *Not* to have a boyfriend because other girls have a boyfriend, but because I value him . . . love him . . . for the person he is. And if I do things the way my mother does, it shouldn't be because she does them like that, but because I've reasoned out that that's the best way to do them! Oh . . . I don't know . . . perhaps I'm not making myself clear.'

'Yes. You are.' He touched me gently with the rackets, as if they were an extension of his arm, and smiled. 'You're pretty good at making speeches! You ought to be in the House of Commons.'

'If I was, I wouldn't say things just because the Labour Party or the Conservative Party thinks I should. They're the biggest conformists of the lot, politicians.'

His smile grew broader. Which made me feel dangerously soft towards him. 'You're getting away from the point,' he said.

'We ought to respect and look up to Mark and Donald as much as anyone else in this school! Not persecute them and ignore them! They've made a stand for individuality

– for their own, and therefore if you think about it – everyone else's!'

'Sssh!'

I wasn't raving at the top of my voice, but I suppose I was talking more loudly than I needed to. Miss Evans, our R.E. teacher, scuttled by like some small, furry animal trying to avoid a storm. 'She's about as individual, that one, as a Lyons' chocolate cup-cake,' I said, quietly. We both laughed.

'Fruit cake?' Brian suggested. 'No. I don't think so.'

'Mark probably knows a lot better than we do who he is, what he is, where he's going. I want that knowledge too, Brian. I don't think I have it yet. A bit . . . but not enough.'

'I asked Keith if he'd told anybody. He had, of course . . . Pat. She'd told her brother. At which point the trail goes dead.'

'We've got to find out who this lunatic is! Before he does any more harm.'

'Is that a condition of us getting back together?'

'No.'

'Well . . . in that case . . . will you come out with me this weekend?'

Ted concentrated pretty hard on *The Nun's Priest's Tale* that afternoon. His monologue was virtually without pause; no asides, jokes, reminiscences, just non-stop explanation of the text. At the end of the lesson, he told Mark and me to stay behind. When the others had gone he handed me a piece of paper. 'The address on that is my address,' he said, and he blew his nose loudly. 'I'd be . . . what's the word? . . . honoured . . . yes' – he grinned – 'if you'd both come round for a drink. And your brother as well, Helen. Tonight? Is that possible?'

We nodded.

'Seven thirty?'

'Drinking with your English teacher!' Mum exclaimed, as we ate our tea. 'How odd!'

'Why's it odd?' I asked.

43

'It's . . . just . . . odd!'

'Don't let him make you drunk,' Dad said.

'I shouldn't think there's much hope of that!' I answered.

He turned to Donald. 'What's the matter with you? Nothing to say for yourself? Face as long as a fiddle, I see. Has she broken your heart?'

'Nothing's the matter,' Donald said.

'Who?' Mum wanted to know.

'Who what?' was Dad's reply.

'*Who's* broken his heart.' Donald got up and left the room, his pork chop, potatoes and cauliflower abandoned on his plate, half-eaten. Mum was astonished: '*Now* what have I said?'

'Teenagers,' Dad informed her, in tones of mild disgust, 'are up one moment, down the next. You never know where you are with them.'

'Is something wrong? Something at school?'

'Not that I know of,' I lied. 'He didn't do well in a test this afternoon. That's all.'

'Spends too much time on the football pitch,' Dad said. 'Still . . . all work and no play.' He looked at the clock. 'I think I can just about fix that wobbly leg on the lounge table before *Coronation Street* begins.'

Mum went to the door, and shouted, 'Donald! Come down and finish your tea! It's getting cold!'

FIVE

Ted's house – small, cluttered, Victorian – was in a pedestrianised street; 'I'm part of the gentrification process,' he said. 'This terrace used to be working men's cottages. The whole area has been spruced up now: hanging baskets, window-boxes, tubs out on the cobbles with the flowers all free, provided by the Council. A socialist Council too! This terrace is occupied by teachers and journalists, even hairdressers; not a labourer in sight these days. The wheels of fortune. . .' Gentrification or not, Ted's living-room was very pleasant, so much so that I made a mental note of this detail or that: I'd do likewise when I owned a living-room. Then I remembered what I'd said to Brian that morning – I wasn't going to have blue curtains because Joanna did. Extraordinary, I said to myself, the contradictions that existed in one's character! Would they ever get straightened out? If they did, was that, finally, being an adult? 'What do you want to drink?' Ted asked. 'Beer, scotch, white wine is the choice. Reasonably unlimited in quantity.'

'I like scotch,' Mark said. 'But perhaps it's a bit strong for now.'

'Nonsense. After the day you've had, I should think you need something strong!'

He was persuaded. Donald opted for beer, and I chose wine.

'That's lovely,' Mark said, pointing to the picture over the mantelpiece.

'A Braque still life. A print, of course. Sheer coincidence – my cheeseplant there and the jug on the shelf,

45

they're more or less reproduced in the picture. I only realised that a week ago.'

The room was fully of such happy coincidences – the pitchpine table and the cane chairs in harmony with the colours of the walls and the pattern of the carpet; books, houseplants, pottery, glassware blending into a neat, lived-in whole. No absent-minded professor's house, this. 'Do you live alone?' I asked.

'Ah.' Ted smiled. 'A question the kids at school never venture. Yes . . . I live alone, but that wasn't always the case. Drinks all right?'

'Yes, yes, thank you,' we said.

'A question the kids at school frequently do venture – of each other, that is: is Ted, or *isn't* Ted? Well, strictly for your ears only, Ted is, was, and ever more shall be so. I bought this house with my lover, Alan. We were sitting on the sofa one evening three years back – this sofa – watching TV, and he said, "I don't think I'm feeling too well." I held him as he lay dying. It took five minutes. A brain haemorrhage. He was thirty-three.'

'That's awful,' I said. '*Awful!*'

'Yes. But eventually I made my peace with it . . . and decided I didn't have room in my life for someone else. Apart from which . . . where would I have met him? I thought I was too old for the pubs and clubs and discos that have sprouted up all over the place these last few years like mushrooms; they weren't around when I was young, of course. There were many compensations. Books, the kids I teach, my garden, travel, friends, dinner parties, this house, music . . . but I was wrong. Of course I need somebody else. Perhaps I've found him . . . I don't know yet. I came to terms with the loss of Alan one evening when I was on holiday in the Greek islands, looking at the sun going down over the sea. Drinking gin and tonic, and dressed only in shorts it was so hot; my legs stretched out on the railings of a balcony. It was probably the gin . . . but I said to myself, my right leg – I'm sure you'll want to laugh at this – is as much a miracle of creation as the sunset. Its functions, and its beauty – if indeed it has any – are, of course, with every minute that passes

46

declining. But, nevertheless, it is a miracle. My me-ness, my self-ness, is a miracle! I've had this sense ever since that . . . that the point and purpose of Ted wasn't only to be one half of Ted-and-Alan, but also to be *Ted*! That being Ted is *good*! Shame Gerard Manley Hopkins isn't on your syllabus; he had a great deal to say on this subject. I like Hopkins; I like teaching him. I love those lines in *As kingfishers catch fire*:

Each mortal thing does one thing and the same:
Deals out that being indoors each one dwells;
Selves – goes itself; *myself* it speaks and spells;
Crying *What I do is me: for that I came*.

Which is what you two – Donald, Mark – are saying and being, aren't you? What I do is me: for that I came. Oh yes, I've been aware of you both . . . for months!'

'How on earth could you?' Donald asked.

'I haven't spied or pried. And you haven't been indiscreet. I just . . . knew.'

'Now the whole world knows.' Donald lifted his hands in a gesture of despair.

'I don't really want to discuss what happened at school today,' Ted went on. 'There are more worthwhile things than that. Paint can be scrubbed off. The culprit may be caught or not be caught – the latter is the more likely, I guess. The world has a full quota of the mentally sick, alas. And though everybody's prejudices came crawling out of the woodwork today, they'll eventually go back in again now they've had an airing. Life goes on.'

'What is more important,' Mark asked, 'than this morning's events at school?'

'You. Donald. Mark-and-Donald. I fear . . . that Mark-and-Donald may be damaged. Not have the nerve to go on. As if it had been attacked by some disease.'

'I have the nerve.'

'That was obvious when you put your arms round him in front of two hundred amazed adolescents! Shock, horror, probe! I'd never have had the courage, but . . . believe me . . . it can't possibly hurt you in the long run. It will be respected. As well as that, you did something important for every kid there who's potentially gay or bisexual. There are others, you know . . . they could be helped by that gesture for . . . for a lifetime!'

Mark, blushing and disconcerted, quickly finished his scotch. 'You're making too much out of it,' he said. 'What do you mean, there are others? Who?'

Ted stood up to refill the glass. 'Not for me to say. But . . . to the point: has Donald the nerve? Can *he* stand the strain?'

'Ah . . . yes . . . well. . .' Donald said.

'We have discussed this a bit,' Mark interposed. 'But. . .'

'But what?' Ted asked.

Donald took a deep breath. 'Maybe I haven't got the nerve,' he said. 'I just thought . . . perhaps we shouldn't see each other for a while . . . till things settle down. I've lost so much . . . friends . . . and there's the football team; imagine what it will be like in the changing-room. . . My instinct is to bolt. Run away.'

'Where to?'

He swirled the beer round in his glass, then swallowed it. 'I don't know,' he said.

'There isn't anywhere you can run to.'

He was silent for some moments. 'Can we change the subject?' he asked, eventually.

'No,' Ted replied. 'But you can help yourself to another beer.' Donald did so. 'Friends, you said. What friends? If they're incapable of accepting you, then they weren't worth having to begin with. But there's Mark. Your sister. Me. Isn't all that quite something?'

'My parents too,' Mark said.

Donald shifted his ground. 'I can't bear the thought of school. Walking through those gates. . . Christ! Another day like this one!'

'Then don't go to school,' Ted said. 'Have a week off.'

'How can I do that? I couldn't possibly tell *my* parents any of this . . . I have to leave the house in the morning, go back after school. . . What would I do with myself in between? Walk the streets?'

Mark laughed. 'That could earn us some money,' he said. 'Good! At least I've made you smile!'

48

'You can come here,' Ted said. 'Who do you have for registration? Mrs Johnson, isn't it? I'll talk to her. You can have the house key . . . and work in this room.'

'Work?'

Ted laughed. 'You didn't think I was encouraging you to take a week's holiday, I hope! You aren't ill, Donald. No . . . you can do your school work here. I'm sure Mark will find time during the lunch-break to come round and see how you're getting on. What do you say?' He fidgeted vigorously with the back of his neck.

'Thank you,' Donald answered. 'Thank you.' He smiled again, but his face was no reflection of his usual, uncomplicated, happy self. The eyes were still full of hurt; the mouth was turned down, its frequently stubborn expression slack, miserable, tired.

'You're not going to do anything silly,' Ted went on, somewhat relentlessly I thought, 'like running away?'

'There's nowhere to hide.'

'And you certainly aren't going to stop seeing each other, I trust.'

'No. Of course not. You're right – that was a stupid idea.' He slipped his hand into Mark's, and rested his head on Mark's shoulder. I looked at Ted, wondering for a moment if he would consider two boys being affectionate in front of their English teacher was going too far – but his face showed no disapproval. His neck remained unscratched and his eyebrows were still.

If Ted's plan that evening was to boost Donald's confidence, it certainly worked. Not that my brother was bounding with his usual zest for life: that didn't happen till months later; but his will to go on was stiffened. As we walked home I was very aware, despite the darkness of the night, of the strength of feeling between him and Mark. I began to have some inkling of how they fulfilled each other's emotional needs, though this created more puzzles in my mind than it solved mysteries. Donald had appeared to be so ordinary in nearly every aspect of his existence; his ability at sport and his enthusiasm for it – he never objected to the knocks, injuries, and mud of the games field – and his competitiveness I had invariably regarded as typically male. He had never rebelled against any of the constraints or expectations demanded of boys, and his friends were of a similar stamp. But with Mark his was not the strong, dominant role; it was as if there was a yearning in him to be soft, tender – feminine almost. Feminine? Did masculine and feminine, with all the conventional meanings of those words, apply in a relationship between people of the same sex; did they correspond to the assumptions in a relationship between people of the opposite sex? I didn't know. Nor did I understand Donald's sexual needs. Why? Simply – why was he attracted to men?

That is a question, I imagine, which doesn't have an answer. Perhaps it doesn't require an answer. We don't ask why we are heterosexual. We just know we are. We accept it and get on with it; Hopkins's 'What I do is me: for that I came.' Was it something to do with his upbringing; Mum or Dad, or both of them, had unwittingly caused it? But I rejected that idea as soon as it entered my head; it was nonsense: if it was true, then I would also be gay.

'You puzzle me,' I said to them. 'But I like it.'

'Nothing wrong with an enigma,' Donald answered.

'We like it too,' Mark said.

Saturday was a good day, the best I think since before that foggy afternoon in the park when Donald first told me. Bitter February weather that had been; it was now almost April, and, briefly, warm and spring-like. Mark borrowed his parents' car and took us to the sea; then in the evening I met Brian and we patched up some of our differences. Mark drove us to a remote, rocky beach near Newhaven and we had it to ourselves: the weather, surprisingly, had not brought out the crowds. The sea was rough, the surf white and glittering in the sun. I sat on a rock and watched it for ages – a beach is the only place I know where I can sit and do nothing; the whole of the self seems satisfied: the ear is lulled, the eye full, and even smell, taste, touch record only pleasant sensations. The sea soothes, heals; it is like a hospital.

Mark decided it was warm enough to sunbathe. He found a private stretch of shingle out of the wind, took off most of his clothes, and fell asleep. Later, as if he'd read my thoughts, he said, 'I'm feeling satisfied. Calmed.' Donald, however, was more restless than we were. His afternoon passed – profitably, he told us – in ambling about the beach picking up stones, peering into rock-pools, climbing a cliff. He laid out his stone collection on the shingle beside Mark; they formed two separate shapes or patterns. 'What are they?' I asked.

'Signs of the zodiac. His and mine.'

'I can just about recognize Leo,' Mark said.

'And Libra,' I said. 'Balance. Have you got it back yet, Donald?'

He nodded. 'Today I have.'

'I shall be nineteen in August,' Mark said. 'School over and done with. I can't wait! Ready to go to university. Free at last. Adult!'

'And I shall be eighteen in September,' Donald said. 'Thirteen months behind him. I'd leave school tomorrow if everyone would allow me.'

'Ted would drag you back by the scruff of your neck.'

'What will being away at university do to you and Donald?' I asked.

'Nothing very awful,' Mark said. 'We won't permit it. Donald, why don't you come here and lie down with me?'

'In front of Helen?'

'You've seen me lying on a beach with Brian,' I said. 'You've seen me kiss him. Did you object? No, you didn't. So what right have I to think you shouldn't do the same?'

Donald smiled. 'My sister is going through a liberated phase. She is enjoying it.'

'Yes, I am. What's wrong with that?'

We arrived home at seven o'clock. Mark ate with us, and afterwards he and Donald went out. Mum thought this very peculiar. 'You told me *you* were going out this evening,' she said.

'I am. Brian is calling for me at a quarter to nine.'

'Brian!' She was astonished. 'I thought. . .'

51

'You thought I was going out with Mark.'

'Well . . . yes. . .' She seemed disappointed. Maybe Mark *was* better-looking than Brian, though when I thought about it not more attractive to me. Mark had become a friend, as Joanna or other girls were my friends. I couldn't see him now as sexy, a boy in *that* way.

'Oh . . . I'm playing the field,' I said. 'Trying to keep them all guessing.'

'Hmmm.' Mum didn't approve. 'You can do that once too often,' she said. 'If you have several boyfriends on the go, you'll lose the lot. You'll end up on the shelf, like your poor Aunt Margaret.'

Aunt Margaret was my mother's elder sister. She had never married, a state of being that Mum considered worse than having a child out of wedlock. Warning me that I'd end up like Aunt Margaret was always her ultimate condemnation. 'There's a long time to go before I need to think about shelves,' I said. 'I'm only eighteen, for Heaven's sake!'

There was a knock on the front door: Brian, half an hour early.

We went for a drink in a quiet pub by the river, then strolled along the towpath. A warm spring night. 'Are your parents friendly with the parents of any of the other kids at school?' he asked.

'I don't think so. In fact I'm sure they're not.'

'Good.'

'Why?'

'I thought . . . some people might have heard about what happened. The lewd wall-poster, I mean. It's just possible that someone has told their mum or dad –'

'Mark did.'

'Well, there could be others less sympathetic, and gossip spreads like wildfire. There'd be problems if *your* mum and dad found out.'

I thought about that for a while, then said, 'It's unlikely.' Few kids would have mentioned such a thing at home, and no parent visiting the school would have seen the messages and drawings on the wall. They had been paint-ed out the morning they'd first been seen; the Headmaster had got the caretaker onto that as soon as Assembly was finished.

'I'm no further forward in trying to find out who's responsible,' Brian said.

'Well . . . you've tried.'

'Are we . . . together again?' He stopped and put his arms round me.

It felt good: his kisses, warm and gentle, roused me much more than those of some boys who were all tongue and thrust and pretended passion. My liking for Brian, my respect, had returned. And tonight I thought him marvellously attractive, even though I said I didn't care for the way his face glistens where he shaves. The brown hair, the dark brown eyes. His voice.

'It's warm, but not that warm,' he said. 'I'll have goose-pimples in a minute! We could go home, but . . . I'm not sure if the house is empty.'

'Shall we . . . see if it is?'

Later, when he was walking me back to my house, he said, 'Have you asked yourself what this maniac could do next? I think we ought to keep an eye on Donald when he's alone.'

'What for?'

'I wonder . . . do you think it could lead up to some kind of assault? A fight?'

I felt a shiver of apprehension. 'God! No!'

'It's possible.'

'But he's almost never on his own! He and Mark are virtually inseparable, particularly since it happened. Anyway . . . why shouldn't Mark be the victim? Why Donald? He's not exactly a weak-kneed twerp! He's tough . . . stronger than Mark is, physically.'

'I know. It's weird. He just doesn't somehow exude a feeling of strength. He isn't macho man. There's something I can't explain about your brother that's very vulnerable.'

Brian was right. But I couldn't explain it either, beyond thinking that it had some connection with Donald almost parading his hurt, whereas Mark hid his, or didn't worry about it so much, or had conquered it.

SIX

Donald's first day back at school was not, he admitted, as appalling as he had feared. But it wasn't exactly a marvellous experience, either. His teachers were O.K., he said; they carried on as if nothing had occurred, as if he hadn't even been absent. Only Mrs Johnson mentioned his week off. 'Are you better?' she asked at registration, pretending for the benefit of the class that he'd had flu or something. Ted told us that this attitude of behaving as though everything was quite normal was a policy that had been deliberately adopted. The Headmaster had called a meeting of the whole staff to consider the matter. Some of this was devoted to speculation about the identity of the paint sprayer, and suggestions as to what to do with him if he was caught, but most of it was spent on a discussion of Donald's and Mark's relationship.

'And a great impertinence that was too,' Ted said. 'We don't have staff meetings to look into whether Helen makes love with her boyfriend or not, and, if she does, should we tell her parents.'

I giggled with embarrassment, and said, 'I'm glad about that!'

'My own view is that if boys and girls are found doing it on the school premises then we have to take some action. Otherwise it's not always our business. The same rule should apply to homosexual kids. Fortunately this view prevailed . . . but it was a close-run thing.'

'What did people say?' Donald asked.

Ted blew his nose, scratched his neck, and raised his eyebrows, nearly all at once. Then he grinned. 'I don't think I ought to tell you who said what. But some fairly unhelpful opinions were expressed . . . such as wicked Mark might be seducing innocent Donald, that it was unhealthy, that you both might influence – or even persuade – others to do the same . . . that it was a sin and the Bible condemned it –'

'That would be Miss Evans.'

'No, it wasn't, as a matter of fact. Then there were those who reminded us that it was illegal, and we had a duty to discourage people from breaking the law . . . one person said you should be counselled by a priest or a doctor . . . another even said you should both be expelled . . . oh, it was a great display of ignorance and imperfection! Fortunately the Headmaster is a moderately enlightened man. He said that no one had proved it was true and that no one *could* prove it was true, therefore he was against doing anything . . . not the best of reasons, perhaps, but it helped to carry the day. I think as the meeting went on he convinced himself of other arguments . . . anyhow, when he asked for a vote on it, nearly everyone who had *not* spoken supported the idea of behaving as if nothing had happened. The silent majority, you see, really is silent most of the time. It's always a vocal *minority* in human affairs that deludes itself into thinking it represents everybody else!'

But Donald did have problems at school from the other kids. None of the teachers, in his absence, had said anything to their pupils concerning how they should react or behave, apart from Ted, who had repeated his lesson on the Housman poem with Donald's class and told them that to send a man to 'prison' 'for the colour of his hair' was inhumane, indecent and disgusting. Clearly not everybody in the Lower Sixth agreed. Though Donald found he was tolerated, even by the sports enthusiasts like Gary, Jake and Andy, he was not welcomed. No one was openly rude to him now, but he was, on the whole, ignored. This still happened to Mark, but Mark refused to let it bother him.

Brian did not follow the general example. I'm not totally certain whether he made himself suppress his prejudices about homosexuality in order to please me, or because he

55

grew to be convinced that the way Mark and Donald were being treated was unjust. He said it was both – mostly the latter. Whatever the truth, he sought them out at school, spent time with them, and when he was at our house he made sure, if Donald was in, that he went up to the attic for a chat. This did not lose him any friends: was a model others might have copied, but they didn't. 'Of the two of them I much prefer your brother,' he said. 'Maybe I feel more at ease because he *is* your brother. Or . . . I don't know . . . I guess I'm comfortable with guys who are into sport.'

'Mark's a games player,' I said. 'A pretty good one, too. On the tennis court.'

'Yes. But he doesn't care any longer. He thinks all that's beneath him, that he's into higher things.'

'He's got other interests to occupy him now. It *is* 'A' level year, you know.'

'Same for me. And for dozens of others – you.'

'Don't I know it! I've got this awful French translation to do for Ernie Pitt – I don't even understand the title!'

I did understand, however, what Brian was saying about Mark. Mark was very self-assured, aloof almost, which to some degree was an admirable strength; but it could be misinterpreted, grow into a source of resentment. People called him a snob. It wasn't that: he just knew his destiny wasn't with the straight crowd of beer-drinking, muscle-flexing males. I mentioned this to Ted, who said, 'Mark's future friends, I guess, will be women and gay men. As mine are. And as Donald's will be, when he's come to terms with losing the heterosexual sporting mob.'

'But why does that have to happen?' I asked. 'Why are there these barriers?'

Ted shrugged his shoulders. 'That's how it is. You know, I admire the women's lib movement. I'm very pro-feminist. But I think the world's in greater need of men's lib. Most men are neanderthal in their basic attitudes! It isn't a question of coming out of the closet; straight man has never really come out of the cave! Women's lib, gay lib: most men feel threatened by any attempt to structure

56

society in a different way from what is traditionally regarded as normal. A challenge to their status, their jobs, the assumptions on which they've always acted. Saying homosexual relationships are good, permissible, acceptable, is implying that marriage and two point four children isn't the one goal everybody should be aiming for. It's casting doubts on male dominance. Men on the whole don't like that! There is one area, however, in which I do sympathise with them.'

'What's that?'

Ted, embarrassed for a moment, blew his nose; then he said, 'Would you be happy if men were allowed into women's changing-rooms?'

'I certainly would not!'

'Why?'

'Well . . . it's obvious . . . I'd feel very ill at ease with dozens of men watching me get undressed!'

'It's understandable, therefore, if heterosexual males feel bothered about gays in similar circumstances. What I'm trying to explain, Helen, is why prejudice is strongest in sport. Explain? Wrong word. I'm hazarding guesses. What I do know is that Donald can't live openly in both worlds. But he'll have to find that out for himself.'

The phantom graffiti artist had not struck again: nothing on blackboards, no further paint on walls; and we wondered what he was scheming next. Or did he think he'd said and done enough? Though I had told Brian that Donald and Mark were virtually inseparable, there were times when Donald was alone; Mark didn't always hang around at school waiting for him to finish a football game. Occasionally I worried about what Brian had mentioned – the possibility of physical attack – but I dismissed such thoughts. Brian is an it-could-occur-and-sometimes-it-does person, but I don't upset myself with imaginary worries, and I invariably refuse to ruin Sunday by thinking depressing thoughts about Monday; in other words I'm a cheer-up-it-may-never-happen type. So when it did happen, it was for me all the more of a shock.

It started in the changing-room after a football practice. Donald, emerging from the shower, and not able to see properly for a moment because of the steam, bumped into Gary. They were both naked. Gary reacted like a dog who suddenly and inexplicably turns on a person it has known all its life, snarling and showing its teeth. 'Watch it!' he said. 'You watch it, you bloody pouf!'

Donald flared up instantly. 'You just say that again!'

Gary did. Then Jake and Andy seized Donald from behind, and pinioned his arms and legs. 'Come on, Gary!' Jake cried. 'Hit him while you've got the chance!'

The rest of the team crowded round, but nobody came to help Donald. 'Let me go!' he shouted. 'Let me go!!' His struggles were useless.

'I'll hit him all right,' Gary said. 'I'll hit him where it hurts, so hard he'll never bother anyone ever again!'

'What's the matter with you?' Donald yelled. 'I've done nothing!'

'Oh. So coming out of the showers and touching me up is nothing, is it?'

He hit Donald, not where he said he would, but in the solar plexus. Donald was winded, gasping for breath. Then two more punches in the face. The door was banged open: 'What the hell's going on?' a voice shouted. It was one of the P.E. teachers, the first eleven coach, Paul Timms. Jake and Andy let go of Donald and he sagged forward, onto his knees. Blood flowed from his mouth and one eye was already beginning to swell.

'Don't move, any of you!' Mr Timms barked. 'I said *any* of you!' Some members of the team were trying to shuffle away. 'Now Gary, would you kindly explain what this is all about?'

'He touched me up,' Gary answered, jerking his hand in Donald's direction.

'That's a very serious charge,' Mr Timms said. 'But . . . if he did, does that automatically give you the right – aided and abetted by everyone else, no doubt – to bash his teeth in? Headmaster for you, immediately after Assembly tomorrow morning.'

'But –'

'Don't you argue with me, boy!' Gary was silent. Mr Timms pulled Donald to his feet, looked at him a moment, then touched the swelling under his right eye. 'You'll live,' he said. 'Go and wash your face, and when you've done that, report to my office. As for the rest of you – get your clothes on and get out of here. Any boy in this building in five minutes' time will also be interviewed by the Headmaster tomorrow morning. And I can tell you right now that when he's heard my tale he is *not* going to be in a generous mood. Not one bit! He won't be thinking in terms of simple little punishments like ten-thousand-word essays or picking up rubbish in the playground for the next six weeks.' He raised his voice and pointed. 'Out!!'

Only Gary hesitated. 'Sir –' he began.

'OUT!!!'

Donald spat a considerable quantity of blood into the nearest basin, and found one of his teeth was loose. He could hardly see out of his right eye. He staggered to Mr Timms's office, groped for a chair and sat on it, then pushed his head between his legs. He thought he was going to faint. After a while, when he felt a little better, he looked up; Mr Timms, who was staring at him, said, 'Drink this – it's brandy. For medicinal purposes and emergencies only. We keep it in the first-aid box.'

Donald drank. It made him gasp and splutter. 'It feels like fire!' he moaned.

'Good.' Mr Timms's face was completely unsmiling. There was a long silence before he spoke again: he was waiting for Donald to recover. 'I'm not going to ask you any questions about what happened just now,' he said. 'I think I can come to my own conclusions about that. Despite what I've heard recently, I'd imagine it fairly unlikely you'd be groping another boy in the showers. Not, at any rate, with the rest of the team standing around.'

Donald glared at him. 'I wouldn't do it at all!' he shouted.

'O.K. I shouldn't have said that.'

'I bumped into him. You can't always see clearly in there. Two weeks back he'd have thought nothing of it! Made a joke about it!'

'I'm sure you're right. Just as I'm sure he is not the graffiti expert, either.'

'No. Of course not! He wouldn't do a thing like that.'

'What would your reaction be if I told you I want the Headmaster to deal with him very severely?'

'Is it necessary?' Donald pleaded. 'There's no harm done. Why punish him at all? I can understand why he –'

'Least said, soonest mended, is it? Listen to me, my lad, and listen carefully. Far too much has been said for anything to be mended overnight. I suppose you think if we allow him to get away with it, you can continue to buy your place in the team!'

Donald was shocked. '*Buy* my place. . . ?'

'Once you had a place you deserved. It was yours by right. Not any more.'

'What . . . do you . . . mean?'

'When you bumped into Gary just now, what did he say? Anything?'

'I'd rather not –'

'Oh, I'm sure you wouldn't! But I'm *ordering* you to tell me!'

'If you must know . . . he called me a bloody pouf.'

Mr Timms looked thoughtful. 'And what do you feel about that?' he asked.

'Well, according to his lights, I suppose I am!'

'So you think you can be in the team, go to practices, play in the matches, put up with that sort of abuse, get the occasional black eye, and everything's hunky-dory? Donald, I am dropping you. As of now.'

'But . . . that's not fair . . . that is not *fair*!'

'I know it isn't. It's the nastiest thing I've done in years to a talented young striker. But there isn't any fairness in this world. Learning that is part of the growing-up process. Do you want to know why I'm doing it? My job with this team is turning all the individuals it consists of into the best team I can make. Capable of winning football matches; that's its point, its purpose. I can't have any disruptive influence in that group of boys. I can't have someone there who upsets everyone else. It destroys the team! The day that garbage was painted on the wall was the end for you. Who did it, or whether it was true or not, is neither here nor there. If the other boys can't work with you . . . then you have to go. Simple as that. I'm very, very sorry . . . because, yes, it *stinks* of unfairness.'

'Oh . . . fuck! Fuck *you*!!'

'For once in my life,' Mr Timms said, 'I'll let a kid get away with that.' He leaned forward, and spoke now in a friendlier voice, more that of a counsellor trying to make a client see sense. 'Donald . . . listen . . . whether you wanted to or not, you have come out – or whatever the expression is – as gay. Perhaps been forced to come out rather than doing it voluntarily, but it doesn't really matter which. You have, as it were, made a big statement. An unpopular one. An uncomfortable one. Most people don't like it; *I* don't like it, and this football team doesn't like it. As I've told you, my job is to get the best team possible. I have to respect some of their wishes. You are dropped.'

'O.K. I understand.'

'I hope you don't bear any malice.'

'Mr Timms. . .' Donald stood up, shakily, and walked to the door. Then he said, 'You bet I bear some malice!'

'Not, I trust, against me, personally.'

'Against you most of all. *Sir!*'

Mr Timms stared at him, greatly surprised. 'Get out,' he said.

SEVEN

Something had to be said to Mum and Dad about Donald's black eye, and the fact that he needed to see a dentist about his loose tooth. He had got into a fight, we told them – that was all: these things happen. But with whom, and what about, Mum demanded. She had a good mind, she said, to go up to the school first thing next morning and complain: why should *her* son be in danger of losing a tooth? Where had discipline and supervision gone? Why weren't the teachers around to stop this kind of behaviour? In the staff room, she supposed, with their feet up, drinking tea. It was time someone made a stand; why should honest, decent boys like Donald be victimised by bullies and thugs?

It looked alarmingly possible for a while as if she *would* go up to the school and complain. Donald and I frantically searched for watertight reasons to stop her, but we couldn't think of anything at all. It was Dad who unexpectedly came to our rescue. 'Calm down,' he said to Mum. 'Did you ever hear of a school where there wasn't a fight once in a blue moon? Don't tell me it didn't happen when you were young.' He turned the pages of the newspaper he was trying to read. 'Yes, it's extremely stupid for boys of Donald's age to get into a fight. Should have grown out of that years ago. But I think you'll look a bit silly if you start lecturing that Headmaster about your gigantic seventeen-year-old hulk of a son being bashed up.'

'Too much of it goes on these days,' Mum said. Her tone of voice, fortunately, was a bit less belligerent.

'Too much of everything goes on these days, according to some people,' Dad answered. 'Let's change the subject.'

It was changed for her by the arrival of Mark, then, a moment afterwards, Brian. The presence in our house of the two young men she assumed were competing for my affections obviously gave her something else to consider; she didn't know how to cope with both of them at once, so she quickly retired to the kitchen: 'I must sort out that freezer,' she said. Mark, Brian, Donald and I went up to the attic.

'So what do I do now?' Donald asked. 'I want my place back in the team.'

'Nothing you can do,' Brian said. Mark and I agreed.

'Huh.' Donald sat on his bed, shoulders hunched, staring at the wall; the very picture of depression.

The Headmaster did not punish Gary at all severely; he limited himself to a lengthy telling-off for hooliganism, and that was that. Perhaps he thought anything more stringent would make the situation vis à vis Donald much worse. Donald had to share the same classroom with Gary, Andy and Jake, but the sending to Coventry now worked in both directions; he had no more wish to speak to the three games players he had once called his friends than they had to speak to him. Donald wanted to do as little as possible at school now. He did the work required of him as adequately as he needed to, but he gave nothing to the school's social life. He spent his spare time there with me, Brian and Mark, and Ted was the only teacher he would talk to more than was absolutely necessary. Other kids spoke to him when they had to, but conversation was merely on the level of what book should they take to the Geography class, or what exactly did Mrs McLellan want done for History homework. Donald seemed driven by a slow-burning anger these days.

The graffiti specialist did not strike again, and we heard nothing about his possible identity. What the Headmaster was doing, if anything, to discover who it was, we had no idea. Donald's tooth was fixed, and Mum and Dad remained completely unaware of the dramas that had occurred. Mark, they assumed, was no longer my boyfriend; he was now a friend of Donald's and they didn't see anything suspicious in that, despite him not being in the same year at school. The one thing we couldn't conceal was that the first eleven had a new centre forward. 'I can't pretend I haven't been dropped,' Donald said. 'I can't take my kit to school and bring it back clean. Or deliberately rub it in the mud so it looks as if it's been used – that would be ridiculous.' Dad was amazed when he heard. Paul Timms, he said, should have his tiny mind examined; no one could exceed Donald for skill and dedication. What was the problem in that school? Standard of the teaching staff, its judgement, its ability, had obviously gone right downhill over the years.

Ted, sensing that Donald and Mark could now cope, withdrew a little from us. Perhaps he thought evenings at his house drinking scotch were not to be encouraged except in the most abnormal of crises. He seemed to be more interested in my 'A' level chances than in Donald's welfare, which, I suppose, is what he was employed for, even if it made me a bit discouraged: the hole we had driven through the barriers between teachers and pupils I considered a good thing in itself, regardless of the particular circumstances that had led up to it. Why shouldn't teachers and their sixth-formers socialise out of school from time to time? It would probably help schools to operate much better than they do.

Easter came and went. Now it was the summer term: last-minute revision, then 'A' levels. Donald-and-Mark were a constant, something settled and reliable throughout the turmoil of the exam period, and beyond. Perhaps I had thought, initially, that they would be a flash in the pan, a temporary aberration, that Donald would get over it quickly, laugh at himself and begin to go out with girls; but I was quite wrong: it was as intense and here to stay as any of the seemingly permanent relationships that flourished in our school. I got so used to it in time that, if I'd heard they had seriously quarrelled or split up, I would have been astonished and saddened. I became convinced, too, of something Donald had insisted on ever since he first told me – he was one hundred per cent homosexual and perfectly happy, despite events, to be so. These things began to seem normal to me, just as it seemed absolutely correct to continue, for now, to hide the truth from Mum and Dad – who never thought it strange that he spent so much time at Mark's house, or that he often stayed there overnight on Fridays and Saturdays.

Brian and I continued to see one another, though I didn't think so seriously now that he was the boy I would eventually live with or marry. The four of us occasionally went out together. Never to a disco: barriers again. There was nothing to interest Donald and Mark at an ordinary disco – what they would want to do most, dance with each other and feel free to touch or kiss, wouldn't be possible – and no amount of persuasion could get Brian to venture into a gay disco. His attitudes to gay life had altered, but taking part in it he could not bring himself to do. He might be seen by a friend, he said, or he might be importuned: he'd drop dead with embarrassment. Our evenings out, the four of us, were to the cinema, to a pub, and on one occasion to the theatre. With two couples there are often two conversations going on, and so it was with us – me talking with Brian, and Donald with Mark; or me with Mark, and Donald with Brian. Never Brian with Mark. Straight males, Ted had said, are still in the cave. Not quite true of Brian – but he was sitting in its entrance.

The morning before my last exam, Mark and I saw Ted in conversation with Tom. 'I'd like a word with you two in private,' Ted said to us.

'The trouble with Helen,' Tom said, 'is she won't make a decision. Should it be this one, or should it be Brian?' (He had, curiously, decided that there was no truth in the stories about Mark and Donald: they couldn't be gay because they weren't effeminate.) 'She needs marriage guidance counselling.'

I laughed: it was said without rancour.

'Interesting news,' Ted said, when Tom had gone. 'We've caught the graffiti specialist. In the act, it would seem.'

'Who?' we both asked, simultaneously.

'Ian Ross. Fourth year. What do you know about him?'

'Nothing,' I said. 'Never heard of him.'

'Ross. Ross,' Mark said. 'Did he have a brother in our year who left school . . . oh . . . ages ago?'

'Yes. Colin Ross. When he was fourteen, Colin was in trouble with the police for soliciting men in public toilets. Bad background: mother committed suicide; father's a long-distance lorry-driver who's frequently away from home – sometimes he left the two kids to fend for themselves for days on end. When the police picked Colin up the social services looked into the matter, and the result was both boys were put into care.'

'But . . . what's that got to do with painting obscenities on the school wall?' Mark asked. 'Why does the younger brother have it in for Donald and me? I don't know him! Don't even know what he looks like! And I'm sure Donald doesn't either.'

'Some obscure revenge because the police caught Colin?' Ted suggested. 'I don't know. I'm not a psychiatrist. The soliciting, it was said at the time, was because the boys needed the money. The father would go off, apparently, without giving them enough to buy food. Though Colin might have said that, of course, to get sympathy.'

'How did you catch Ian?' I asked.

'I didn't. It was Miss Evans. She came into school three quarters of an hour earlier than usual; some work she had to correct before first period – she'd forgotten to take the books home with her yesterday evening. She went to her room, and there he was, drawing on the board. Nothing obscene this time, though the usual heart with the drops of blood and the arrow. And your name, Mark, and Donald's. The message was: "I would like to wish all my readers a happy summer holiday." '

'What did she do?'

'She spotted at once that the writing was identical with that of whoever had painted the words on the wall. Ian, when he saw her, immediately tried to rub out the evidence, but she grabbed hold of him, twisted the rubber out of his hand and threw it across the room, then quite literally frogmarched him out into the corridor. She locked the door behind her – she wanted the Headmaster to see the blackboard, she said, as proof it was done by the same person – and propelled Ian up to the office, his left arm still in a half-nelson.'

'Miss *Evans* did all that?' I said, amazed.

'Very difficult to imagine,' Mark said.

Ted grinned. 'She really is *not* the little mouse you kids all seem to think she is! In fact she's a very tough old bird. An ex-Cambridge hockey blue, and she once thumped a burglar unconscious with a poker. Her favourite Biblical quotation is "And Jesus said, I come not to bring peace but a sword."' He laughed. 'You always stereotype your teachers! You imagine that in private life we're the same as we are in the classroom. You'd be astonished at the extent to which we're not!'

'What will happen to Ian?'

'He isn't going to be punished in the usual way, of course – an hour's detention and told not to do it again would hardly be appropriate! The social services and the education office have been informed, and . . . we wait and see. Oh . . . I expect they'll put him in a special school and have him psychoanalysed. Much good that will do!'

'Does Donald know?' Mark asked.

'Yes. I was teaching him first thing this afternoon.'

'How did he react?'

'He went pale and said just three words: "I'll kill him!" Mark . . . he obviously won't, but . . . please make sure he doesn't do anything stupid.' He paused, scratched his neck, and blew his nose. 'Well,' he said, 'I think that's it. Term ends on Friday . . . have a good time this summer and keep in touch. Make sure Donald in particular enjoys himself . . . he needs to.'

'I will,' Mark said. 'Don't worry.'

One of the good times that summer was returning to the beach we had visited that Saturday months ago; on this occasion Brian came with us. The weather was hot, almost a record for August, the experts said. The sea was crowded with swimmers, and we soon joined them. It was difficult to keep out of it for long, though I declined Mark's invitation to go with him, Donald, and Brian for a fifth swim; I wasn't a mermaid, I said. I sat on a rock and enjoyed myself just watching, though the waves weren't as rough, white and glittering as on that previous afternoon. When he emerged from the water, Mark decided to sunbathe. Donald did not potter about collecting stones. He wasn't so restless now: he lay down beside Mark and relaxed. The discovery of who had written on the blackboards and painted on the wall had lifted some of his depression; calmed him. He hadn't killed Ian Ross, of course, nor attempted to; he did, however, after Ted had told him, hurry off to find Ian: 'I just wanted to see what he looked like,' he said to me. 'I wanted to fix his face in my memory. It's a rather ordinary face, not particularly evil. Scared rabbity eyes, and a weak mouth. Do you know . . . I actually felt sorry for him!'

Brian didn't feel sorry for him. 'Little bastard deserves all he gets,' was his comment. He stayed on the sand with Mark and Donald for a while, then strolled over to my rock, put his arm round me, and stared at the sea. He said: 'You can feel a bit left out when you're with those two.'

'*I'm* here.'

'You looked so engrossed I didn't think you wanted company.'

'Ah! Poor Brian!' I teased, and made a little bit more room for him on the rock. 'It's a funny old world, isn't it!'

'Yes. Odder than I'd thought. But why do you say that now?'

'I don't know. I was wondering how long everything lasts. Whether you and I will be together longer than Mark and Donald.'

He looked disconcerted. 'I'm not sure I like the sound of that,' he said.

'The sea makes me think odd things. It's all flux, never still for a moment.'

'We'll last if we want to last.'

'Yes . . . and I'm sure *they* will.'

These events happened two years ago. Jason Smith and I went out to dinner with Ted recently, and in the course of the conversation I told them I had ambitions to be a writer. 'You've got a subject,' Ted said, 'and the characters. Also the plot, and something important that needs saying.' Since then he's been phoning me, badgering me to get on with it, just as if I was still in the sixth form. I guess teachers *never* stop teaching.

Mark got excellent 'A' level grades, and went to the University of Sussex to read for a degree in English. Donald was determined to follow him there, and he did so, a year later. He's studying History. They share a flat in Brighton, and are about as happily married as any two people I know. Donald has taken up football again, and Mark complains about dirty games kit on their bedroom floor almost as much as Mum did. Things turned out differently for me. I, too, got a university place, at Bristol, but when I go to Sussex for a weekend, it isn't Brian I share the sofa-bed with at Donald's; it's Philip, a man I met at a party a few weeks after I left school. My relationship with Brian just fell to pieces. When I last had news of him, he was working for an electronics firm in the north of England and living with a woman called Hazel, some fifteen years older than he is.

I often urged Donald to tell Mum and Dad. 'I will one day,' he said. 'I'm not ready. And they aren't, either.'

'I don't like the pretence,' I said. 'The secrecy. The lies.'

'I may be nineteen, but I'm not even legal yet. The law says I'm still supposed to be a virgin.'

'Oh . . . this daft under twenty-one business.'

'Yes.' He grinned. 'Not that it ever stopped us, right from the start. And the same is true for thousands of others, I guess. We live in an absurd world.'

Dad discovered the truth one day by working it out for himself. 'It's odd,' he said to me. 'Donald's best friend

69

turned out to be a boy in a different year at school. If it was a girl, I'd understand that. Very few women in Donald's life.'

'Oh, he'll meet a nice girl,' Mum answered. 'Settle down and marry her. He's just waiting till he's finished his studies.'

'I don't think so,' Dad went on. 'I wouldn't be a bit surprised if they were . . . Donald . . . Mark. . .'

Mum, who was sewing a button on a shirt, paused, needle in mid-air. 'Go on,' she said.

He turned to me. 'What do you know about it, Helen?'

'Me? You'd better ask *them*. It's not my business.'

'So I'm right. I've been wondering . . . for a long time.'

Silence. It lasted a full minute. Mum and Dad just stared at each other. Then Mum returned to her sewing. 'I've always known,' she said. 'I just didn't want to think about it. I guess Donald imagined I wouldn't see that picture on his bedroom wall. But I did see it.'

'What picture?' Dad asked.

'Mark.'

Dad stared out of the window. 'Weather's clearing up. I'm going down to the pub.'

'To the pub!' Mum was alarmed. 'You haven't been in a pub for years!'

'Well, I'm going now. Don't worry . . . I'm not starting all that again . . . drinking. I just need a little pick-me-up.'

'Dinner will be ready in half an hour.'

'I'll be back.'

'He's buying me a car,' Mum said, when he'd gone. 'A Fiat . . . so I don't need to get a bus to work. It's red. You did know I'd got myself a part-time job, Helen?'

'I'm amazed!' I said. 'It's incredible! Why aren't you freaking out?'

'I am . . . you see . . . used to the idea. Though we didn't call it gay back then. Your Aunt Margaret . . . that's why she never got married.'

Extraordinary people, my parents.

PART TWO
1986

ONE

The Syrian desert, a rhinoceros hide; and the pilot had just announced that Amman was half an hour away. Why was he going there, Mark asked himself, not for the first time. There was only one place that occupied his thoughts: Camden Town. Where Donald was in bed with another man, maybe even now, this minute, this second, coming. Nausea of sexual jealousy: a seizing in the muscles like paralysis, so akin to the urge to vomit it always surprised him he did not actually throw up; then the overwhelming desire to hit, to hurt, to smash.

He started to write a letter. 'My love – I'm flying! It's a marvellous sensation! I can't imagine now why I was ever frightened of the thought. How I wish you were with me, sharing it all; I miss you so much there are no words to convey the depths of missing you. Perhaps, when I've –'

Why was he writing such rubbish? Donald would throw it into the wastepaper basket. Or laugh, and read it aloud to his lover.

Hands round Donald's neck, strangling. I'd never get away with it, he thought; that's the problem.

He tore the letter into several pieces.

Months previously, Rick had said, 'Are you going to tell him?'

'No. Oh, I suppose so.' Then, 'I don't know. I don't know what there is to tell.'

'What do you mean?'

'I don't know what I mean.'

Rick, sensing that Donald disliked even the mildest of pressures in this direction, was silent. But puzzled: that

73

Donald had ceased to love Mark and now loved him was obvious. Not, of course, the easiest of matters to break to one's lover, even a lover of a month's duration, and those two had been together for ten years; but it seemed to be more than the simple facts of the case that bothered Donald, something other than being the cause of pain and suffering. 'I must go now,' Rick said. He got out of bed and dressed.

Alone, Donald sat staring gloomily out of the window at the canal. Clouds, trees and water were the same oppressive grey. And the silence of the flat, disturbed only by the occasional traffic noise, was even more oppressive and sad than the grey outside. I hate it here, he thought; I hate it! A cage, a prison! But . . . where do I go? And why?

It was true that he was not in love with Mark; for months had felt only boredom, had not in any way been turned on by his lover in bed. It had happened before, these patches of tedium, but where there had once been the will to see them through and come out the other side in a greater degree of closeness, there was now an overriding desire for release, a longing to experience the pleasures and vicissitudes of Donald alone. They had been together too long, mutually dependent, almost symbiotic. What was this Donald, the mature adult male; had it ever had a chance to find out who it was without Mark shaping, moulding, influencing it?

Rick was of no importance, a catalyst merely, a trigger. A university student, charming but inexperienced, who lived in the next street. Donald had met him in the Cage aux Folles. He provided not only the sexual attraction and excitement that Mark seemed without, but also the novelty of a relationship with somebody younger, one in which Donald, for the first time in his life, was teacher, initiator. A youthful body, blue eyes and a wide smiling mouth: Mark, nearly twenty-nine, was putting on weight and losing his blond hair. But he couldn't envisage exchanging Mark for Rick, swopping his shared existence with the one for similar routines, domestic, sexual, or whatever, with the other: Rick was a key that turned a lock in a

74

door that would open an enchanted garden, a world the nature of which was as yet quite unknown. Opening that door and looking would not suffice: the garden had to be entered. What was this world? Himself. Exploring it would be the discovery of his real nature, finding out who this Donald was.

It was selfish of course; and how to tell Mark wasn't exactly easy to work out. He was fairly certain that Mark knew he was sleeping with Rick, but tensions between them lay more in matters domestic, the result, Mark probably considered, of Donald's increasing depression about being unemployed. Donald was the home-maker; it was he who usually did the cooking, had the final say on colour schemes and furniture, carried out the decorating projects, but recently Mark had come home from work to find meals uncooked, or the spare room had only two of its walls painted and no attempt had been made to finish the task; covers were unpicked from cushions and not replaced. And had grumbled. Sometimes irritatingly; just because he had a job he seemed to think that Donald, who had not worked for two years now, had no right to flop into an armchair in the evenings and complain of a difficult and trying day. Mark, who worked for a firm of industrial designers, would go on about his problems: the boss was an idiot; the secretaries were two-faced, and what was the point of his creating elaborate advertising lay-out when it wasn't used? Then . . . what was there to eat for dinner? Not another cauliflower cheese! At this point Donald usually felt it was impossible to start a discussion about the difficulties he had had with trying to get through another long day of blank, empty nothingness.

It was time to do something drastic.

Rain: Helen watched it streak down the windows like tears. It was the wettest summer she could remember.

When Mark or Donald, or occasionally both of them together, arrived at the house these days Brian disappeared into the garden or his garage, leaving her to cope. *She* was the sister, the old friend, the fag hag;

they wanted to talk to her, not him. Embarrassed, unable to help and not really wanting to know much about it, he was pleased to escape. But now, in their absence, he was asking questions.

'My brother's mind,' she said, 'when it comes to examining his feelings, just goes flit-flit-flit from one surface impression to another. He's petrified of not being able to understand what he's up to, so he avoids any attempt to think about it at all.'

'You're hard on him.' Brian was lying full-length on the sofa, staring at the ceiling. 'His treatment of Mark isn't totally callous.'

'I didn't say it was. Doesn't the word "callous" somehow imply that you're conscious of what you're doing?'

'Yes.'

'He certainly doesn't take into account anybody else's feelings. I mean he never says to himself I want to do such-and-such, but I won't because it would hurt Mark.'

'Seems rather immature.'

'It is. The last time I saw Donald he said, "I don't know what I'm doing or why I'm doing it." But Mark will survive, I guess. He's a giver, not a taker.'

'Sexually the other way round, I thought.'

'Honestly, Brian! Whatever's that got to do with it?'

He thought for a moment, then said, 'Maybe quite a lot. Perhaps the sex and the emotion never clicked properly.'

'Oh, it did! It certainly did! You should hear them both on that subject!'

He grimaced. 'I'd rather not.'

Helen was amused. 'You've never understood it, have you!'

'No.'

'Donald says the world's divided into two classes of people, chamber-pot users and chamber-pot washers. One group uses them, the other cleans them out. He blithely admits he's not one of the washers.'

'Typical of the way his mind works! Grasping at a plain clear-cut definition when the truth of the matter is

76

so complex there aren't any adequate words to define it at all!'

'Another of his ideas,' Helen said, 'is that people can be classified as dogs or cats. He's a cat. You and I and Mark are dogs.'

'We have this semi-detached house in East Finchley, two children, several goldfish, one smelly rather moth-eaten rabbit, a clapped-out car, and all the usual domestic articles and problems. A dog's life? All we've done is to join the bourgeoisie!'

'Don't forget that we aren't married, and that one of our children is therefore born out of wedlock, while the other isn't even yours. Because I can't be bothered to get a divorce, and somewhere in Europe there's Philip, my husband, who, out of the generosity of his guilt complexes, gave me a house. Which we sold in order to buy this one. No, it doesn't mean we're dogs. Or lead a dog's life.'

'Well . . . we all have to have some differentiating signs, I suppose. Just to make sure we exist.'

'Donald has some childish notion he and Mark can still be friends! Occasionally go out together for a meal, or an evening in one of their pubs or clubs. What that really means is he still hopes he has a life-line.'

'Fuck them both!' Brian said. 'The subject bores me rigid. Come here.'

'Why?'

'Just come here.'

'Yes. O Lord and Master.'

She is more lined than she used to be, he thought, under the eyes when she smiles. The same raven black hair. A calmer person. Self-assured. The maturity shows in the way she thinks and talks, the letters she writes. She's grown almost beyond recognition. 'I think . . . I shall take your clothes off and make love to you on the hearth-rug,' he said. 'For old times' sake . . . and the children are out.'

'Old times' sake?'

'You haven't forgotten, at the age of seventeen on your parents' hearth-rug?'

'No. What would the bourgeoisie say?'
'Retire with their discreet charm behind shut curtains.'
Helen shut the curtains.

A year previously her parents had moved from Croydon to North London; Dad had decided there could be more opportunities for his work, Chris Price Disposals. 'One suburb, Jane, is much like any other,' he remarked cheerfully when Mum was expressing doubts on the subject of living in Tottenham. 'And you'll be much nearer to Helen and to Donald.' It was the nearness to Donald that worried her. Though they both got on well with him up to a point, Donald had an odd effect on his father when they were living in close contact. It was the homosexuality that disturbed Chris; my son, my only son, he would often say to himself in moods of self-pity. The thought of no grandchildren bearing his surname made him feel uneasy. Inferior: it was a kind of slur on his maleness. The fact that Helen had two delightful children seemed to make no difference.

In Mark's opinion, Chris and Jane appeared at a superficial level to accept his and Donald's homosexuality completely, but he didn't really trust them. They needed to be liked too much, needed to impress him with their kindness and tolerant liberalism. Surrounded by his and Donald's friends (Donald's twenty-first birthday party was a typical example) they conveyed the idea – tacitly and not so tacitly – that they ought to be regarded as an intriguing and unconventional couple, admirable in their generosity to a bunch of faggots. He couldn't help noticing in all the photographs Chris took at that party there was not one of him and Donald together. He was certain that if anything went disastrously wrong Chris and Jane would drop him instantly, and welcome Donald's new boyfriend. It was impossible for them to take the relationship as totally serious, however long it might last, simply because it was homosexual. When he and Donald first lived together, the only thing Chris and Jane had given them was an old bookcase that was going to be

78

chopped up for firewood, whereas they were lavish with wedding presents to Helen.

Donald sought his parents' advice when he decided to do that something drastic and leave Mark. They couldn't make sense of his reasons, couldn't grasp the idea that Rick was not just a straight swop for Mark. Donald's vague talk of freedom, of being inside a cage, of wanting to live out of a suitcase and find himself, was alarming. 'The trouble with homosexual relationships,' Chris said, 'is that they don't last. Always end in tears. It's tragic!'

Donald looked at his mother, but she said nothing. She would compromise in any way to avoid argument: Chris had been drinking steadily again for some years. 'Not all heterosexual marriages last,' he said. 'And you can't say yours has been absolutely smooth.'

'More credit to us,' Dad answered, 'for making it work. Particularly when it seemed to everybody else that it wouldn't last five minutes. Well . . . if it's all over, you make sure you get that watch back.'

'What are you talking about?'

'The watch you let him wear. He's had it for years and it's the property of this family. Belonged to my grandfather. You make sure you get it back.'

Donald winced. 'Yes, Dad.'

Chris stood up and smiled. A heavily-built Falstaffian man: truculent and disturbed now, but at other times charming, the life and soul of any party. 'I'm going out,' he said, and, intercepting his wife's anxious look, added with more emphasis than was necessary, 'to put some water in the car radiator.'

Jane said, when he had left, 'Bring Rick over here one evening. I'd like to meet him.'

'Yes, maybe I will,' Donald replied, without enthusiasm.

'Donald . . . what *is* wrong?'

He was silent for a while, then said, 'Maybe I could move in here for a bit. Till I get myself sorted out.'

'Of course. Any time. We'd love you to.'

79

Mark's discovery of the truth occurred one day when he came home early from work, feverish and unwell: a stomach upset. He went to the bathroom, wondering if he was going to vomit. A few minutes later he heard Donald arrive at the flat with Rick; though they knew he must be somewhere nearby because his car was parked outside, they made no attempt to behave with any discretion. 'I'll see you in the morning,' Donald said eventually, 'as soon as I can make it.' Rick left.

Mark's heart was thumping uncomfortably and he felt dizzy; never before had he overheard his lover having an orgasm with somebody else. Donald came into the bathroom, naked, and said, 'I thought you must have gone out for a walk. Are you O.K?' He looked guilty and frightened.

'Yes.'

'Sure?'

'Of course I'm sure. Are you having an affair with Rick?'

'No.'

'Don't lie! Have you had sex with Rick?'

'No.'

'Look at your hands. And your cock.'

'Why?'

'I'm old enough to recognize sperm when I see it.'

'Yes, then. If you insist. But nothing . . . important.'

'Are you in love with him?'

Donald steadied himself before answering, and said, trying to look Mark straight in the eye, 'I don't know. Sexually, he turns me on . . . fantastically.'

'You mean you don't enjoy making love with me?'

'It's different.'

'How, different?'

Donald, a slight crossness in his voice, said, 'Do you remember the first words I ever spoke to you? Years ago in the school changing-room? You were putting in one of your rare appearances in that place, and you were being teased about the huge size of your balls. As big as plums, I remember thinking, and they *dangle*. I said, "I envy you, a pair like that." That's what it's been about ever since!'

'I don't understand a word you're saying.'

'Sex! I'd been dying to have a cock shoved up my arse since I was thirteen! I used to wank myself senseless just thinking about it! And you wanted to shove it there! Oh, it was fantastic, certainly; I couldn't get enough of it. Nor could you. The way we trembled and groaned and begged each other to stop; we were coming, coming, coming! On one occasion my sperm actually hit the ceiling! But you would talk about love and ecstasy and love again –'

'This is all lies. You're rewriting history.'

'You made me feel it was only permissible if it was love; that's what I resent! You talked me into thinking it was there when it wasn't . . . all that jelly-like, quivering emotion! When really it was screwing. Why couldn't you ever think of it as just two boys giving each other gorgeous sensations with their hands and mouths and cocks and arseholes?'

'You're only saying this so you can leave me more easily.'

'Perhaps. All right. Yes. There was love, I suppose. Yes, I did love you. Once upon a time. But I'm so *bored* with you now! Every time I want sex, you're at the ready, like . . . like a tom-cat on heat. Where's the fun, the hunt, the chase, the thrill? It's gone!' His voice rose to a shout. 'Didn't ever exist!'

'You'll get AIDS.'

'Not if I take the right precautions.'

'And do you?'

'Yes.'

'Where's the condom Rick's just used?'

'On the bedroom floor.'

'So Rick, with a rubber, is preferable to me without?'

'Yes! A thousand times yes! It's exciting, and wonderful, and different! Mark . . . I'm leaving you. For good. Christ! I didn't want it to turn out like this! But I'm going! I must, I must! I must be free of this place, of you. . . How I hate this flat! This . . . this jail sentence! We've been together so long and since we were so young I just don't know who I am or what I'm capable of, and I've got to find out! I'm going, and I'm going now!' He turned

81

and went into the bedroom, got dressed, then pulled two carrier bags out of a cupboard and started to fill them with clothes. Mark followed him from room to room, watching, astonished. Donald opened the front door.

'Donald. . .' Mark raised his arms, gently.

'Don't touch me. Please.'

A thin light drizzle had begun, grey shawls and veils of it drifting along the street. Donald walked off, in the direction of Rick's flat.

Where he stayed for a month. The worst month, Mark was able to think later, of the whole messy revolting procedures of break-up. It was the geographical proximity that was so hard to accept, so . . . unkind. It meant he was constantly aware of Donald's movements; it would have been much easier if his lover had emigrated to the other side of the earth or just dropped dead. For it was worse than a physical wound or a bereavement; it could not heal, was made to fester daily, almost hourly. Though Mark could not see the flat from his bedroom, it was only just out of sight. He had to pass it on the way to work, and he usually knew whether Donald was there or not, for Jane lent him her car, the now elderly red Fiat. This car became an obsession for Mark. He would spend hours driving around, looking for it; and on two occasions he nearly caused what might have been a serious accident through not paying proper attention to the driver in front. Why he wanted to find it he couldn't really fathom: just to see them together? Make some kind of dramatic fuss? But he rarely saw it, not even outside the nearest gay pub, the Black Cap, haunt of many of their friends: perhaps Donald was ashamed of the gossip that might ensue. Mark thought people regarded his relationship with Donald as a paragon. He was proud of their respect, needed it. It would wither. He did not want to be one of the unattached, frequenting bars every night; wallflowers in his opinion, secretaries thrown back into the typing pool, while Donald happily enjoyed moving at once into another affair: and the break-up, he thought, would spread a sense of unease, remind their friends of the jibes of straights that homosexual relationships were in their very nature shallow and brittle.

On the day he told Ted Viner what had happened, he saw them. He'd met Ted for lunch, and was driving him back to Victoria when the Fiat turned out of a side road just ahead; Donald's arm was lying along the top of Rick's seat, his hand stroking Rick's neck. Mark skidded to a halt. Ted got out of the car: 'Move over,' he said; 'I'll drive.' He drove up to Hampstead Heath, and they looked down on London. It was a rare, warm day: hazy sunshine, cloud shadows moving slowly across the rich pattern of grass, woods, water, and the grey structures of the city.

'People have lived here for over two thousand years,' Ted said. 'Don't think your suffering is unlike anybody else's.'

'I don't. But that doesn't make it better.'

'It's your city too. You've roots here. Don't let yourself be hustled away from it.'

'Fuck the city! Fuck roots!'

Ted did not answer, but took him to the car and drove to Croydon, to his own house, which he now shared with Jason.

They plied him with so much scotch that he had to stay the night. He slept, anaesthetised by the alcohol. Usually he didn't, despite taking valium before he went to bed; it worked, in that he would fall asleep easily enough but woke after a few hours, and finding the other half of the bed empty, he would be instantly awake, two a.m., three a.m., no warm body of Donald breathing a heart-beat away, and he was quite unable to sleep again. Sometimes he lay there till sunrise, still too shocked by the hurt even to think. Once he got up and finished painting the spare bedroom. But mostly he would go out and aimlessly drive the car or walk the streets, hovering by Rick's house if the Fiat was parked there, and wonder which of those darkened rooms his lover and Rick were sleeping in.

Over the years he had at times become bored with Donald in bed, but he had not indulged in any adventure on the side. Sometimes he flirted with other men, and knowing that a few might sleep with him if he asked, he would say to himself, why am I doing this? He didn't want it: there was, really, only Donald. He remembered one occasion at a disco being very attracted to a beautiful blond boy, the best dancer on the floor, and having talked to him, discovering that sex would be a possibility, and dancing with him to *If I can't have you, I don't want nobody, baby*, he realised that the song said: if I can't have *Donald* I don't want nobody. And he said no to the beautiful blond.

To think that he meant nothing to Donald, physically, not just at this moment, but for ever, was an appalling blow to his self-esteem. Would everyone find him unattractive now? Was he simply unattractive, period? One of the worst aspects of gay life, he said to Ted, was that it was so youth-orientated: slim young bodies, unlined fresh faces – so many people valued them more than stability, love. His waist-line was bigger; his hair receding: for some – many – gay men he might just as well not exist.

'What shit he talks!' Jason said, when Mark had driven home on Sunday morning. 'Why should he think stability with a man who doesn't love him preferable to a condom and a beautiful boy for the night? Why does he think we look on his relationship with Donald as some exemplar of virtue? It isn't. Never was! Why does he have to ape heterosexual patterns all the time?'

'He can't face the idea of being alone,' Ted answered.

'There are two things I want in a lover – a body that turns me on; and if we have to part we part as friends. If you live together it presumably helps if you like doing similar things, and can respect each other's space when you want to be by yourself. All the rest is so much crap, and the crappiest crap is looking for someone else to give you security. Like all neurotic obsessions it's a self-fulfilling prophecy – you end up getting precisely what you're afraid of most. It's time Mark grew up.'

'Oh . . . big speech!'

Jason grinned. 'Tell me this,' he said. 'Why on earth is it I find complete happiness living with a man who's old enough to be my father? Who put me in detention when I was twelve because I'd forgotten to do my English home-work? Who wouldn't lay a finger on me – because he was dead scared – until I'd left school, even though he knew I was dying for it and was madly in love with him?'

'Luck,' Ted said. 'The sheer chance of things. And . . . if I remember rightly . . . I didn't keep you waiting that long.'

TWO

'But how did it happen?' Helen asked.

'He rang me up at work, and suggested we go out for a meal –'

'Which you paid for, I suppose.'

'– and we had this amazing, fabulous, unbelievably great evening!' Mark laughed, and looked out of the window. 'Then we went back to the flat and made superb love. Yes, love, not sex. I'm not so stupid nor so inexperienced that I can't tell the difference! I don't remember anything like it for months. I almost said years . . . but that wouldn't be true. And he's still there, in the flat. A week now! Though . . . it isn't the same. I don't know what's wrong: he won't discuss things as we used to. He's very depressed. But he did talk about Rick. It was such a relief to find I hadn't been replaced, if you know what I mean. I begin to be sorry for the boy! He became too insistent, Donald says; too clinging.'

'The one thing Donald keeps reiterating, the one little fixture in all the confusion whirling about in his mind, is that he doesn't want a relationship: no ties, no responsibilities. With *anyone*.'

'I don't understand you. He's *there*!' Mark said. 'What's he doing, then? Just doesn't feel like going to your parents' house, doesn't feel like making the effort to get a place of his own, so he plumps for the easiest solution?'

'Yes.'

'Why . . . it's *evil*! Has he been here? Has he talked to you?'

Helen poured herself another drink and sipped it before

answering. 'Mark, I won't be a post office where you and Donald mail letters to each other.'

'But. . . ?'

She was silent for a while, then said, 'The usual talk about the need for freedom.'

'Freedom! What do we do with it? Ability to choose signifies being adult, doesn't it? People normally choose to share their freedom with somebody else.'

'Not everyone. Ted Viner didn't, for ages.'

'That was simply his defence mechanism after Alan died! I've heard him on that subject a dozen times! Anyway . . . he and Jason are now an old married couple. They've been together nearly as long as Donald and I have.'

'Perhaps Donald doesn't feel he's an adult yet.'

'At almost twenty-eight!' Mark exclaimed. 'That's nonsense.'

'You've been lovers since he was seventeen. I don't deny you've given each other room to grow and develop enormously. But how many adult choices have you made on your own, Mark?'

'Not many, I suppose.'

'Donald feels he's made none. He thinks that if he is to develop any more as a person he's got to make choices unhindered by you. All right, you may say that's absurd, but it's no use just *telling* him that!'

'You think he won't stay long, then?'

'Hasn't that crossed your mind as being . . . probable?'

'Oh yes,' he said. 'Yes. It has; I've got to admit it. A few days ago he went on about our bedroom being so gloomy. Well, he decorated it himself the year before last; *he* chose the colours: it's not *my* fault. I didn't have any say in the matter. I asked, is Rick's bedroom very different? So light, he said. So light! The light of one's life? Anyway, I've just repainted it, this week. Threw out that awful old carpet, did the walls cream, stained the floorboards. . . Maybe I was trying to see into his mind, how he would do it if he were doing it now. And he said it was far more beautiful than anything he could imagine . . . but it was the peculiar way he said it. Looking at the

87

walls like a visitor. As if he wasn't going to see them again.'

'He doesn't want to be accountable, doesn't want to have to fit in round your needs and concerns. Sex with you . . . it's not the same. It's the staying the night, every night, waking up beside you each morning . . . it's a trap. *He* thinks. He can't see that within the context of a relationship it's possible to have almost all the necessary freedoms. It's that "almost" that bugs him. He can't compromise, can't give. Don't you think on the whole he's the one who's done the taking?'

'Yes, I do. And it didn't matter. My love was in the giving.'

'That warm, protecting, caring love . . . that's what he finds so . . . repellent.'

Her words hurt, enormously. 'Why the hell can't he talk to *me* about his problems?' he said. 'What's so wrong with *me*? *Why*?'

'Perhaps he fears you'd talk him down. Or out of it. Persuade him he's wrong.'

'He *is* wrong!'

'Mark . . . there have been other men . . . since he's returned. . .'

'In our bed? When I've been at work?'

'I didn't ask for the details. But there'll be more. You're going to have to face a time that might be worse than Rick. He might come home to you at night; he might not. If I were you . . . I'd tell him to fuck off out of it.'

'I can't do that.'

'Why not?'

'Because I love him,' Mark said. 'I don't respect him; I don't believe him. I don't mean he deliberately tells lies . . . well, he does sometimes . . . I mean he lies to himself. Constantly! But for me there's no one else. There can't ever be anybody else. I *love* him! I have no options.'

'He doesn't love you. He can't possibly love you, whatever he may say, and treat you as he does. And you *do* have options.'

The truth of it all was so evident, he said to himself. So utterly obvious! And he had driven to Helen's, eager to tell

88

her the good news that Donald was back, that everything might now be the same as it had always been. He'd come alone because Donald was meeting his father in the Jack Straw's Castle. Or was that another lie? He glanced at his watch – ten to eight. He was supposed to be picking Donald up at half past. 'I must go,' he said, abruptly.

Donald was not in the Jack Straw's Castle.

'Mark. My parents' home is my home. In a sense that's always been true. If I have any roots that's where they are.' They were eating dinner at a little restaurant in Highgate; the clientele was young, all of them younger than they were. That's why he chose it, Mark thought; this perpetual need for youth. It's sickening. Donald had moved three days previously into the spare room at his parents'.

'Did you only want dolls' houses?' Mark asked. 'Playing with cookery books and colour charts? Adolescent games?'

'I'm certainly not domesticated any more. The whole syndrome – I hate it.'

'Why?'

'I don't know.'

Mark sighed. What were they doing here, he asked himself; what on earth was the point? Such meetings could only stop him from taking any positive action in the direction of mending the broken pieces of his life. Donald had moved his possessions out except for his furniture, and, though they had argued over such things as who should have the electric mixer and the gardening tools, they had on the whole managed with a stiff politeness, sometimes even moments of warmth. 'Oh, you might as well take the mixer and whatever you want from the garden,' Mark said. 'I shan't bother to use the bloody things!' Donald, grateful, kissed him. And when it was time to leave he was unable to let go of Mark's hands. 'We'll meet in a day or two and have a meal together,' he said. 'I'll be in touch.' So Mark stayed indoors, waiting for the phone to ring instead of going to the pub or to Ted's or Helen's, even refused an invitation to a party.

'I suppose you're a lot better off at your parents' house,' he said. 'Money has been a problem these past two years, hasn't it? It's caused too many tensions between us. Me earning and you unemployed.'

'I don't intend to stop there long. I must find my own room.'

'So you can invite all your men back.' Donald said nothing. 'You don't mean Chris and Jane allow it?' Donald looked away, and gestured impatiently. 'Good God, they do.' He swallowed his wine in one gulp.

'I didn't want to tell you because *we* never did. Just another hurt. I'm sorry!'

'Yes. It does hurt. And your mother giving you an almost totally free hand with her car so you can get to the pubs and clubs and whore around. How can she do it?'

'What do you mean, how can she do it?'

'Does she ever think of me?' Mark asked. 'What damage it causes me?'

'She is worried about . . . what I'm doing to you.'

'Oh, yes! With the top of her head. I know her! Her one concern is Chris's drinking. Anything to maintain the balance, to keep the home on an even keel. I count for nothing. I never did.' There had been a crisis in his relationship with Donald when they were both still at Sussex. Donald had gone through a stage of being impossibly clinging, jealous and almost manically possessive; he would rush home hours before he said he would arrive, expecting to find Mark in bed with another boy, and there was never anybody else, not even a hint of a passing trick, let alone a lover. He made fearful scenes when Mark spent five minutes just talking to a friend or an acquaintance who, he imagined, was a threat; and babbled away to his father about Mark preferring other people's company to his own: Chris, very drunk, plied him with alcohol, and said to Mark, 'Give the boy security! Give him the security I've never been able to give him!' As if it was a serum to be injected into the bloodstream, not something Donald could only find inside his own self. 'He's left home. He's not my responsibility now! Oh, my son! My only son! I wish . . . we were able to help you!' He wept into his gin; then grabbed Mark's arm and twisted it till it hurt. 'If anything happens to him, if he goes off the rails, I'll seek you out . . . and cut your right hand off!' Mark broke free, and, trying not to lose his temper, appealed to Jane. 'Leave my missus alone!' Chris shouted. 'It's nothing to do with her! Pestering her when she has enough worries! Oh, my son, my son! My son is a faggot and my daughter married an imbecile! Where have we all gone wrong?'

'You're very quiet,' Donald said.

Mark awoke to his surroundings. Poppy's, a restaurant in Highgate High Street. 'Let's have some more booze,' he said.

'Are you paying for it?'

'I thought we were going halves on this meal.'

'I'm sorry.' Donald looked glum. 'I can't. I've no cash.'

'Write a cheque.'

'My overdraft's too big. I'll pay next time; I promise! We'll go to that new bistro in Gospel Oak . . . the one you said you wanted to try.'

'Where Arnold works. Been there recently?'

'Mmm . . . yesterday.'

'Someone took you out to dinner?' Mark asked. 'Slept with him as payment? Back home in the bedroom next to Chris and Jane?' Donald lowered his eyes. 'Well, I wouldn't screw you tonight for love or money; that's for sure! I won't be one of your tricks! I'm *Mark*! Remember me?'

'Don't shout. People are staring at us.'

'Who was it?'

'Don't be ridiculous.'

'*Who was it?*'

'Why do you want to know?'

'WHO WAS IT?'

'Sssh! If you must know . . . Arnold himself.'

'Arnold! Arnold!!' Mark roared with laughter. 'How *could* you? He's so ugly! That slack mouth and bulging eyes. Hideous! Non-stop superficial chatterer. Did you stick elastoplast over his mouth? The only way you'd get any sleep. And, so I'm told, pretty second-rate in bed.'

'It was all right.'

91

'What are you trying to prove?'

'Prove?'

'If it has balls between its legs it has to fuck you! What a way to find out who you are! Some voyage of self-discovery, Donald!'

'Leave me alone!' He looked at Mark. Vulnerable, but defiant.

Mark's anger collapsed. 'I love you,' he whispered.

Donald's move to his parents' house had a curiously unexpected effect on Chris and Jane; it was not his father who seemed to feel the stress but his mother. There was time to do things with Donald that Chris had not done for years; a trip to an antiques market on Saturday morning, an evening with old family friends, a tour of St. Paul's Cathedral, which neither of them had visited since Donald was a child. 'Dad's as pleased as a dog with a juicy bone,' Donald told Helen. 'It's as if he'd got his little boy back again.' Jane, however, did not easily adjust to having another person in the house; it was too disturbing of the daily routines on which she had come to rely as a solace for her husband's return to drinking. She was fussy and house-proud to a fault; 'living with her is like living in a museum,' Chris complained frequently. Everything had its proper place, even to the point of storing saucepans on precisely the same spot on a shelf; colours had to match exactly: she had recently bought a new washing-up bowl because the previous one wasn't the shade of brown really suitable for her kitchen. She knew her behaviour in these matters was excessive and she could often allow herself to be teased about it; one evening last year, when Mark and Donald had come to dinner, Chris said, 'Mum thinks you've both been sitting on that sofa too long, so she wants you to put the dust-sheet over it!' At the time she had found this amusing, but in periods of tension she was unable to appreciate the humour, indeed became more intolerant in the house, dusting, washing, polishing, hoovering several times a week.

Donald's way of being domestic was not unlike his mother's, something Mark found as tiresome as Chris did.

Gone were the old days of sports kit strewn everywhere. A great deal of his behaviour was in fact modelled on Jane, with whom he had had a particularly close relationship in early adolescence as a result of his father's drunkenness, which had tended to frighten or disgust both of them. When drunk, Chris could be either dangerous or unpleasantly maudlin; crockery would get smashed, food thrown round the place – Helen, as a child, had had ice-cream stuffed into her ears, Donald hot stew poured over his head – or else absurd olive branches were produced: on one occasion Chris, on the way home hours later than expected, had stopped and bought a Japanese tea service, thirty-two pieces in all, which he presented to Jane in the hope of avoiding her anger: 'As if,' she said to Helen, 'I knew thirty-two Japanese well enough to invite to tea!'

But Donald was now suddenly in revolt against any domesticity, especially his mother's kind of fastidiousness; it smacked too much of the sort of permanence he found totally unpalatable. Soon they were at loggerheads. 'Your room is a tip!' she complained.

'It's my room. Or so you said.'

'You do nothing in the house! I cook for you, wash your clothes, do your ironing, and you don't even dry up a knife or a fork! You can't even open the attic curtains when you get out of bed in the morning! I wonder how on earth Mark put up with you.'

'I shan't be here much longer.'

'I never know if you'll be in or out, here to eat a meal or not, if you're staying away all night or –'

'I get the car back for whenever you want it. I've not failed once in that.'

'Only because you know you'll not be borrowing it again if you do fail.' She stared at him. 'You're twenty-seven and behaving like a teenager! Like some irresponsible nineteen-year-old.'

'You've hit it on the head! That's *exactly* what I'm doing: behaving like some irresponsible nineteen-year-old! Why? Because I was never nineteen and doing the things appropriate to that age; I was already into a nice cosy routine with Mark, just like you and Dad. I'm making up

for lost time. Christ! To think how much time I have lost!'
He put on his jacket.

'Where are you going?'

'Out. And I don't know when I'll be back.'

They were half-way through the meal – trout (Jason had
caught it himself) and a bottle of hock – when the phone
rang. 'For you,' Ted said to Mark. 'It's Donald.'

Who was upset, tearful, and incoherent. 'I'm so alone.
Talk to me, please!'

'What's wrong?'

He wouldn't say. 'Can I come over there?'

'No. Where are you?'

'At East Croydon Station.'

'I'll be with you in ten minutes.'

Jason began to sing, sotto voce, *It's a bad time to leave me,*
Lucille. Ted glared at him. Mark apologised to his hosts,
and, abandoning his dinner, rushed out of the house. He
was conscious, as he told them where he was going, of
an expression of amazement on Ted's face, contempt on
Jason's. He has only to lift his little finger, they seemed
to be saying, and you come running. What else can I do,
he thought as he drove off; what else can I do? I have no
choice.

Whatever had upset Donald seemed to have vanished
when Mark arrived. He was no longer tearful; a bit
depressed maybe, but nothing else. And the explanation,
when it came, made Mark very angry. 'I should have
stayed and finished my dinner!' he stormed. 'And told you
to fuck off! I was enjoying myself!' The problem was some
German Donald was sleeping with; this Helmut wanted
him to go back to West Berlin for a holiday.

'I couldn't say yes and I couldn't say no. I kept
hedging. I'd think about it; I'd tell him later. I couldn't
stop thinking, what would Mark say? What would he
feel about it? So much so that eventually I just didn't
know what to do. Helmut . . . he's returned to his hotel
in Kensington. When we said goodbye . . . the look in his
eyes. So hurt.'

'Do you ever think about the look in my eyes?'

Donald blew his nose. 'Snap, and you come running,' he said. He flicked his fingers.

'And it reminds you that you've got me cheap. You disgust me!'

'Sometimes I disgust myself.'

'I'm going back to Ted's. There's a lemon soufflé, which is always delicious when Jason makes it. As you know. I might get the last spoonful.' He pulled out his car keys, and stood up. He felt very aware of being made to look as if he was without the minimum of self-respect he would have hoped to retain, to have been pushed beyond the limit where others would dig in their heels. He was less of a person, he thought, in the opinions of three people: Ted, Jason, and Donald. Lessened, too, in his own eyes. As for Donald's dilemma about going to Berlin: the truth, Mark said to himself, isn't concern for me. He simply doesn't fancy Helmut all that much. He's flattered by the attention, and tempted by the prospect of a free holiday.

'I think of you as I think of a teddy bear,' Donald said. 'Sometimes I want to cuddle you, sometimes I want you in bed with me, sometimes I want to kick you . . . but mostly I want to put you in a corner and forget about you. And I want you to stay in that corner till I need you again.'

'I'm a human being,' Mark said.

THREE

Mark phoned his mother and told her that Donald had left him. She made little comment, feeling too stunned to say anything helpful. A few days later she asked him to come home for the weekend. 'I've told your father,' she said.

'How did he react?'

'Sympathetically, of course.'

When he reached Croydon depression engulfed him so strongly he had to make an enormous effort not to turn the car round and drive back to Camden Town. It was a damp, silent afternoon, the roof-tops hidden in a sea of woolly fog, dull and grey as himself, like those blank years in adolescence before he met Donald, when living in this dreary suburb seemed to strangle him, squash his life to extinction.

Even at the house his parents had lived in since before he was born there was no escape from Donald. Mark had been child and teenager here, had grown up and left; these rooms, his old bedroom, belonging to immaturity, the only bit of his life that had nothing to do with adult relationships, should be the one place his lover could be forgotten. But, like everywhere he found himself, there were memories: in this bed he and Donald had spent their first whole night together.

'You look drawn and tired,' his mother said. She was shocked by his appearance.

'I didn't remember to shave. That's all.' He glanced in the mirror: yes, a bit more pallid than usual, perhaps.

'You've lost weight.'

'Nearly a stone.'

'Are you eating properly?'

'I think so. I never lose my appetite, whatever the crisis. Odd. Most people can't eat when their world spins out of balance. So how have I lost weight?'

'Nervous energy. Are you still unable to sleep?'

'Five hours is about the maximum; sometimes it's no more than two. And I'm not really tired; I get used to it. But how do you kill the time at night?' He yawned and rubbed his eyes, then sat down heavily on the sofa. 'Can I have a drink?'

'There's plenty of scotch. Help yourself. Mark . . . don't do anything silly.'

'I've thought of it.'

'Don't. Promise me!'

He did not reply.

Later, when they had eaten, he went out for a walk with his father. Mr Sewell had retired from work a year ago, and his energies seemed to have dwindled to an aimless kind of pottering: he was always losing things, letters, his pipe, his handkerchief, and he was content to pass much of the day looking for them rather than doing anything of importance. He was, at the moment, unwell; hobbling, even with the aid of a stick: a slight twinge of rheumatism, he said. Nothing to worry about.

They talked platitudes: inflation, Margaret Thatcher destroying the country, the Council spending too much money on unnecessary projects, the need to extend the M23 into London. A retired social worker, Mark said to himself, with a wife and son he loves but doesn't really understand: what has been the point of his existence? It's no better than mine.

'I'm sorry that you and Donald have split up,' Mr Sewell said. 'I really am very sorry. If there was anything I could do to help you, I would. But there isn't, of course; you can only come to terms alone. People always suffer alone: no one can take the burden from you, even share it. If I were you I'd seriously think about leaving London. Make a fresh start. You're young. Your life is ahead of you. Stop making yourself so available. To Donald I mean. Don't see him at all. Finish it.'

'I can't.'

'What will you do with the flat? You're joint owners, aren't you?'

Mark nodded. 'Donald says he doesn't want his half; I can have it. I've paid the mortgage every month since we've lived there; he was unemployed and still is: I didn't expect him to . . . I suppose it's now mine more than his.'

'What about his property?'

'He's moved his stuff to his parents' house, the small things; not his furniture, the dining-table for instance, or his desk. Temporarily, until he's found a place of his own. He's not making much of an effort to do that!'

'Have you altered your will?'

'I tore it up,' Mark said. 'I had an orgy of tearing up, photographs, letters . . . smashing things too: just as well Donald had taken away his precious pottery and glass . . . I . . . took all the records that had any romantic associations for us into the garden and smashed them to bits with a hammer.'

'That was stupid.'

'Yes. But maybe it prevented me from smashing Donald to bits with a hammer.'

Mr Sewell stared at him. 'Have you made another will?' he asked.

'Not yet.'

'Do so.' They stopped and looked at the view. They had climbed the hill beyond the old airport, and could see the office blocks, the spread of houses: grey. The fog was lifting, but the sky seemed to press down heavily. 'It will rain later, despite the forecast. . . You know, I like this view. When we came here thirty years ago, I hated living in Croydon! I felt it was a kind of death. But I've got used to things. More than that; I've grown into the place: it's grown into me. When I retired we thought about moving, a bungalow on the coast at Burnham Overy, Wells-next-the-sea, somewhere like that. But I'm glad now we didn't. I see by the way . . . that you're still wearing Donald's ring.'

Later, alone in the flat in Camden Town, Mark went over this conversation in his head. Dad was ageing rapidly. Was more distant than he used to be. They were growing apart.

Hampstead Heath: reddish gold light on water, lines of cloud green-tinted in the dusk, flocks of birds pursuing their own secretive life, windows glinting with the last of day. The dregs of day, the lees of day, rich, warm, beautiful: Mark, there were some good times, some marvellous times . . . and yet.

Up here on the heath was the most exciting place for sex, the kind of sex that at this stage of his life was exactly what Donald wanted. In the bushes, in the summer dark, the hands of invisible strangers, men whose silhouettes could just about be glimpsed in the blackness, slowly unbuttoned his shirt, undid his zip, thrust his jeans down to his ankles, pressed bottles of poppers against his nose, explored his cock, fingered his arse. It was a fantastic turn-on when four or five of them were doing this to him all at the same time; which would he allow the pleasure of letting him come? Holding it back; moving from one man to another; making it last an hour, two hours, till his legs felt as if they'd been running for miles. Best when he had no idea which mouth he shot in, so long as the poppers were still carrying him into ecstasy, the hands still busy with his arse, legs, balls, tits; and *his* hands and mouth were still enjoying cock, scrotum, balls: selecting the best, the biggest balls, the cocks that tapered up like rockets – thick, firm cocks attached to firm, youthful bodies that shuddered and cried out and came at the same moment he chose to release his own sperm. Totally divorcing his sexual needs from everything else in his nature was, he realised, something he'd always needed to experience, to revel in, if only for a while: to weigh it, assess it, and perhaps find it wanting – perhaps not. It was like examining something in a very pure, unalloyed state. The darkness was a help: the absence of sight increased the power of the other senses, hearing and touch in particular – judging the quality of another man's orgasm depended on listening to breath, to shivers of pleasure, and the hand or mouth alone decided whether a cock

99

was marvellous or not. Eventually, he reasoned, he might choose to put his sexuality back into the rest of his life, better equipped to deal with it in his relationships. Or he might make other choices.

Christ! I needed that, he said to himself as he zipped up his jeans, adjusted his shirt. He walked back to the car and drove to Camden Town. As he neared the flat, he slowed, then stopped. He didn't want to go there at all. There would probably be another heavy scene if Mark was in, but that he could face, that was not the reason: it was the reminder of failure that oppressed him, the half-finished projects he'd abandoned, the inability to cope with the responsibilities of being loved. The disenchantment dated from . . . when? Soon after they'd moved here, and he'd found himself jobless, alone day in and day out? Was it really then? Perhaps, as he'd said, there had never been love at all. Just fucking. Perhaps he'd always used Mark, right from the teenage years: prop, crutch, giver, provider of sweets.

A car passed. The driver waved and tooted his horn: Rick. Why not? That was a much better idea than going to see Mark. He'd been intending for weeks to call on Rick; at least he had been able to split up with *him* and stay friends.

He spent an hour at Rick's flat. He didn't feel like returning to Tottenham, but there was nowhere else to go. The pubs were shut by now; Helmut was in Germany, and the clubs – oh, sometimes it was just too bloody far to traipse into Central London. Of course there were other people he could call on, even stay with till morning; but he began to wonder with increasing frequency why, in some of his sexual adventures, he was doing it. Why, he would ask himself as yet another condom was filled, am I in this man's bed? Hampstead Heath was much more rewarding.

He knocked on Mark's door. It was nearly one a.m. but Mark was still up, ironing a pile of shirts. The record player was on, full blast; as soon as Donald appeared he turned it up even louder as if to say he didn't want any conversation, at least not until the music had finished.

100

Modern: extremely discordant and harsh; Donald didn't recognize it. He picked up the sleeve – the fourth symphony of Vaughan Williams. The blurb said something about a political comment on fascism, an orchestral jeremiad; it spoke of one of the most relentless and implacable marshalling of forces in all music. The tunes (if you could call them tunes) were either cries of passionate protest or deliberately trivial and inane, parodied by gruff contempt from the brass. Moments of hushed false calm, muted strings slithering uneasily from one clashing key to another, led to the Terror being unleashed again: the whole thing, as it reached its grinding climaxes, seemed not so much to speak of chaos, but to *be* chaos, disintegration, the epitome of destruction.

It was over, blown to bits. 'Why were you playing that?' Donald asked eventually, surprised after such a battering that his voice sounded quite ordinary.

'I like it.'

'It's appalling!'

'It's what I feel. So watch it.'

'What do you mean?'

Mark put the iron down. 'Why does your fucking mother have to keep on lending you her fucking car?'

Donald looked at him, frightened. 'It's none of your business,' he said.

'Oh yes, it is my business! You say she's worried about me, but she lends you her car so you can visit your little whore!'

'So you were snooping. Again.'

'I had to post a letter. God, why should I even bother to tell you? The mail-box is down the road and in order to get there I have to walk past Rick's flat.'

'She didn't know where I was going.'

'That's irrelevant! She knows bloody well that when she lends you that car you're off to be fucked by some man or other. I think it's quite incredible she lets you . . . it's *inhuman*! As if I were some piece of discarded rubbish.'

'I did not go to bed with Rick just now! He happens to be a friend of mine.'

'Do I believe you? Does it even matter? Truth, Donald,

to you is the first convenient semi-coherent bundle of phrases that enters your bird-brained head.'

'Don't. Don't! Please.' He touched Mark's arm.

Mark picked up the iron and thrust it towards Donald's face, an inch away from his eyes. 'I could smash this into you. That's how I feel. That's how violent I feel.' He put the iron down. And said to himself, what I really want is to cover you with kisses, take you upstairs and make love all night long. 'Get out!' he screamed. 'Get out!!'

Donald fled. Later, he said to his mother, 'How could he say that and ever have loved me?'

Next morning, a Saturday, Mark drove to Tottenham. At eleven o'clock he was drinking coffee at Tinley's: out of the window, on the other side of the street, was the blackening stone of a church. But he looked with unseeing eyes. Jane, who worked at a shop nearby, had twenty minutes' break at this hour of the day and often came in here.

She was alone, fortunately. 'Mark! I . . . half-expected this.'

'So he told you.'

'Yes.'

'Running home to Mummy to tell her about the savage brute who threatened him.'

'Something like that, yes.' She sat down at his table. And smiled: but her eyes were wary.

'To come to the point. Will you please stop lending him your car?'

'I can't do that.'

'Why not?'

'Why should I? I don't always need it. He's my son. And an adult; where he goes and what he does it not my business. But I have told him . . . to be . . . a bit more discreet.'

'Discreet!' He laughed, then said with heavy sarcasm, 'Thank you, Jane. Thank you very much; you're such a tower of strength! Look . . . how would you like it if Chris was having an affair, and your mother-in-law lent him your car to go and visit his bit of stuff?'

'I shouldn't like it at all.' The waitress approached. 'Coffee, please. Do you want another cup, Mark?'

'No thanks. It's the same though, isn't it?'

'Is it?'

'Oh yes, yes! It *is* the same! Can't you ever realise that?'

'There are . . . other considerations,' she said.

'The fact that we're gay.'

'Of course not!'

'Chris's drinking would go over the top? The bum! I hate his guts . . . I think – quite illogically, I know – that he's more responsible for this mess than anyone else.'

'I do admit . . . we could in the past have helped you, both of you, rather more than we have done.'

'Don't give Donald everything he asks for! Can't you see that it doesn't do him any good?' He was silent, stirring the sugar in the bowl. 'I must go,' he said. And left.

It was not his rudeness that depressed her; that was only to be expected: it was the fact that she was never able to influence events. Both Donald and Mark had told her on many occasions that homosexuality had absolutely nothing to do with early upbringing; they didn't blame anybody for it, they were perfectly happy and at ease being gay. No one knew the causes of homosexuality, they said; after all, who knew what caused heterosexuality? The questions weren't even worth asking. But she remained unconvinced, and recent events, she thought, were proof that she had been right. There was nothing *she* could do about it, however; her existence was devoted to making the here and now work as best it could. It wasn't a dishonourable way of living in her opinion: second-rate, perhaps, but not evil, not immoral. It might all be worse if she behaved differently. But one day, she said to herself, she would astonish everybody by doing something drastic.

Donald surveyed his room. It was a bed-sit off the Holloway Road, a Victorian terrace near the tube station. All right, providing he did not look out at the street too often: red bricks, grey tiles, windows. Shut in and claustrophobic, quite unlike the flat he and Mark had lived in with the canal at the bottom of the garden. Other people's furniture, brown and drab. Lace curtains. The table was covered with a long heavy cloth of worn velvet, and the bed was narrow, essentially for one. All those windows! So many eyes staring. However, the room could perhaps be made into his own. He unpacked his things: clothes, some books, an ash-tray, kitchen utensils, cushions. He shifted the bed, dragged the table away from the window, put some houseplants on the mantelpiece. Then stopped. What was the point? This place could never be home.

This was freedom.

He gazed at a photograph of Mark. An extremely good likeness, taken some years ago; his hair was longer then. In profile: serious, unsmiling. The little finger of his left hand touched his mouth. Donald looked at it for a long time, then shut it away in a drawer. He couldn't imagine why he had brought it with him.

Mark. Hell, no; don't think of Mark. This is me, my room, where I am I, not the lesser partner; here I am free. Get out of my head, fuck you! Leave me alone! What would I feel if I saw you with someone else? jealous, hurt, angry? Mark, come through that door now take me in your arms take me to bed cover me with kisses oh my love my love the only precious thing that's ever happened to me Mark what have I done the memories the sweet dear times you're part of me and that's what I can't stand the prison the shackles oh what do I do with this freedom now I have it tied to me as a tin to a dog's tail our life our shared precious life destroyed smashed torn to bits as you ripped up the photographs and battered the records Christ stop it's madness madness. . .

'Why are you here? Why do you come back so often? You just want to persecute me!'

'Don't be silly.'

They were sitting in the garden, drinking wine. A lazy summer afternoon, insect murmurs, flower scents: on the bank, a white boat without the prop of water had sagged

104

sideways. The canal shimmered in the heat.

'There's too much that's not been right for too long,' Donald said. 'Becoming joint owners of this flat, for example. I think I only agreed because you wanted me to agree. It was easier to say yes than to argue. It's symptomatic: I've been for so long the inferior partner, under your influence, turning into what you wished me to be that I've lost any sense I might ever have had of my own identity. Relying on you more and more for money since we lived in this place: I loathe it, despise it! I *despise* your money! We were much happier when we were students, equals, not having any idea where the next meal was coming from. I don't love you. Not any more. I'm very fond of you . . . I'll always think of you, worry about you, perhaps even be very hurt by you. I can't have a sexual relationship with you now. But . . . I have only happy memories. Superb memories!'

Mark sighed. 'I want to forget that you ever existed.'

'You're still wearing my ring.'

Mark stared at it. A black onyx, set in silver. It was curious that it had not been given to him when he had given Donald a ring; it was two years later, he remembered. He'd hinted, more than once, that he would like a ring, but there had been no response. Yet when Donald decided that the time was right, he spent ages looking for the one that would give the most pleasure, no expense spared. 'He kept asking my advice,' Helen said. 'He arranged to have it altered if it didn't fit properly. . . He was incredibly excited about the whole thing.'

'It's a mockery that it exists,' Mark said. 'Here, take it.'

'I don't want it. It's yours. But it, too, is . . . symptomatic. Or so I think now.'

'What do you mean?'

'I gave it to you because you wanted it.'

'Not because you wanted to give it to me?'

'A symbol of what might have been . . . not what was.'

'So it's a fake!' Mark jumped up and ran indoors.

105

'What are you doing?' Donald shouted, but there was no answer. Mark returned, holding the ring in one hand, a hammer in the other. 'No! No! Don't do it! *Please!*'

He placed the ring on the ground and smashed it to pieces with a blow so hard that the hammer head flew off and sank, without trace, in the canal. 'I swear to God that if I see you again I'll *kill* you!' he screamed.

Donald walked along the towpath towards Camden Lock. To calm down, he told himself, in order not to lose his own temper: at least since leaving Mark he had not once been driven into a rage. He would now have to avoid the places Mark was likely to be, not borrow Jane's car: he didn't want the tyres slashed, a brick through the windscreen. I couldn't live with him now, he thought, I couldn't: I'd be terrified! The ugliness in his character – sweet, gentle, loving Mark; and underneath was that violence, that viciousness! It would be like sitting on a time-bomb.

He drove up to Hampstead Heath. As usual, its own busy life seemed to go on regardless of anything else, was a kind of sedative or distraction: nothing here changed, the white walls of Kenwood, the ancient trees, the sweep of the land, the men hungry for sex. His cock was sucked, fingers stroked his balls; and he did likewise, groped, caressed, sucked. Then he said to himself: I don't want to come like this. I want to be screwed.

Arnold perhaps; he hadn't seen Arnold for a while. Mark's judgement was of course perfectly correct: an idle chatterer, one whose hallmark was verbal diarrhoea. Not even particularly good-looking, but a big cock. A very big cock.

Mark dressed in white shirt and white trousers and went to the Black Cap. He immediately felt out of place, wrongly dressed, and there was nobody at the bar of any possible interest. Boring, boring! Perhaps I'll go into town, he thought; perhaps I'm ready for the clubs: maybe I can stand the music, even if it's songs that remind me of Donald. 'Are we in love or just friends?' he sang under his breath: no, it didn't hurt. Maybe he would meet the most marvellous man in the world tonight; beautiful, fascinating.

But he didn't want to run into Donald, so he decided to take the precaution of driving along the Holloway Road. Yes, the Fiat was parked outside the house; Donald was therefore at home. With a man, or . . . watching TV, having an early night for once?

They met at the bar of the Phoenix. Donald, flushed with drink, was in great good humour. 'Lovely to see you! Are you going to join us?'

'Us?'

'Me and Arnold.' Mark followed him, knowing it was a mistake, but he felt quite unable to do anything about it. Arnold had also been drinking too much: the words babbled on, non-stop, silly rubbish trickling into Mark's ears.

They had been out to dinner. 'I had nothing better to do this evening,' Donald said. 'Arnold paid.'

'How will you pay him back?' Mark asked. 'With your body?'

'Why not?' Donald looked truculent, a bit like his father, Mark thought. 'He's been screwing me most nights this week; why not one more?'

'Who else have you slept with recently?'

'Oh . . . only Neil.'

'Neil! He's bald!'

'Yes. Have you ever been in bed with somebody and thought to run your fingers through his hair, then realised he hasn't any? It's a most curious sensation.' He moved away and danced with Arnold. Why not leave at once? It was the only sane thing to do. Apart from which there was a conspicuous absence of any men here who looked remotely beautiful or fascinating. But he did not leave: something in him was making him respond to the exuberance of Donald's mood; in that, he used to think, lay some of the magic of Donald.

'We must dance to this!' Donald dragged him by the hand. *Catch me, I'm falling in love.* 'I suppose it's golden oldies half-hour. Remember this?' Then, gazing at Arnold, who was alone at the bar sipping beer, he said, 'Shall we get rid of him?'

'Who?'

'Our Arnie of course.' He was silent for some moments, nuzzling his face against Mark's, then he said, 'Tonight . . . I haven't enjoyed myself so much for years.' They kissed. 'No. It wouldn't do. I suppose . . . we'll have to leave you to your own devices.'

Mark nodded. 'I suppose you will.'

'But it's been good . . . really good seeing you.'

'Has it?'

'I feel happy!'

'Happy anniversary, then.'

'I'm not sure what you mean,' Donald said. 'What anniversary?' He laughed. 'It *is* rather funny, meeting you like this. If it's a joke, I wonder who it's against.'

'Not Arnold. Though he does look a bit glum.'

'That's his problem. Anyway . . . I'll make it up to him in bed.'

'The joke's against you. Ultimately.'

The next record was *It's Raining Men*. 'I promised this to Arnold,' Donald said. Mark watched them. There was nothing particularly intimate in the way they were dancing; just a couple of friends. But, he thought, how enormously Donald was enjoying the flattery and attention from *two* admirers!

Half an hour later they said goodbye and left. Mark decided to follow them; there was little point in staying, even though he hadn't been in the club very long. Eyeing up men: a waste of time; he couldn't cope. He drove behind them out of town; Arnold's car was faster than his, and when they reached Mornington Crescent it edged away. He could see their heads growing smaller as the gap slowly widened, and eventually they disappeared out of sight.

It was late, well after midnight; he was at home, wondering whether to go to bed or stay up longer: there didn't seem much point in pursuing either course of action. A sense of disgust with himself, stronger than the feelings of rejection and hurt, began to hit him: if

108

Donald had behaved that evening in a particularly callous and frivolous manner, his own behaviour, conveying the impression that he was enjoying himself, pretending to condone what Donald was up to, was worse. Why had he hidden everything he really felt? It was as if he had no moral standards or judgements, was merely a cipher grovelling before a man who had become a festering lily.

Manhattan Transfer on the record player were singing *Love for Sale*. He listened to it several times, trying to memorise the words:

Love that's fresh and still unspoiled
Love that's only slightly soiled. . .

He switched it off. Perhaps he should read something; there were several books on his shelves he had not read, had bought thinking that one day he would find them of interest. He glanced at the titles: *How Far Can You Go?*, *Between the Acts*, *To Have and to Have Not*, *Undo Your Raincoats and Laugh*. He opened his copy of Housman:

Tell me of runes to grave
That hold the bursting wave
Or bastions to design
For longer date than mine.

Nothing: too near at hand,
Planning the figured sand,
Effacing clean and fast
Cities not built to last
`And charms devised in vain,
Pours the confounding main.

He went into the bathroom. The little medicine cabinet above the basin: why not? He reached for the bottle of valium. There were enough pills here to finish it all. *Why not?* He opened the bottle and emptied it, slowly counted the tablets: yes, quite enough. He carried them into the lounge, placed them on the table and stared at them. Up till this point he had been completely detached about what he was doing, as objective as if he was another person watching himself, or as if he was playing a game

109

like patience simply to pass the time. But when he said am I really going to do it, and the answer was yes, the circumstances changed dramatically. He found himself gripped by a series of powerful emotions quite unlike anything he had ever experienced, physical pressures that seemed to come from outside his own body, as if some force had violated him and was holding him in a state of suspended animation. It took a great effort to move his hand; even breathing was difficult: there were pains in his chest, a blockage in his throat, and his tongue was leaden, too large for his mouth. And the most awful nausea began to attack every part of him, his legs, head, arms, stomach, even his back-bone. He thought he was going to faint. I have only to make perfect my will. He had a fleeting image of last wills and testaments; wondered momentarily what legal difficulties would occur for parents inheriting the property of a son who had died intestate and by his own hand; remembered the pleasure he had felt years ago writing his will, leaving everything to Donald.

'Have you ever been in bed with somebody and thought to run your fingers through his hair, then realised he hasn't any? It's a most curious sensation.' Happy anniversary, Donald. Ted. Jason. Brian. Helen. *Helen!* He couldn't cause her this much hurt. Perhaps he should phone. Why? To ask her forgiveness? It wouldn't be a cry for help. The voice inside him grew in strength: you can't do this; you just cannot do something so dreadful. Eventually he was able to stand up and move across the room. He stared at the telephone. Brian never slept well, always found immense difficulty in sleeping again once he had woken. He would be quite furious if Helen dragged herself out of bed and rushed over to Camden Town at – what was the time? – twenty to two in the morning.

He went back to the table, and looked at the heap of pills. He would wash them down with whisky: there was an unopened bottle in the kitchen cupboard. Someone had told him – Chris, he remembered; how ironic! – that valium and whisky were a lethal combination. It was just a question of time; five minutes, maybe ten, and he would do it. Donald. My life, my happiness! All sunlight and

110

dancing. When we first knew each other and we were apart, that first Christmas, you signed your letters with the word 'Sol.' There is no more sun.

He went to the cupboard and fetched the whisky. Then he picked up a handful of tablets.

Now.

A motor-bike engine. Lights. Footsteps. A knock.

Three days later he was on his way to the Middle East. Jason had planned to go there for a holiday – Amman, Petra, Aqaba: the Arabian desert, the Dead Sea – but his mother had died of a heart attack; as the only surviving relative he had to organize the funeral and sort out the will.

Mark bought the ticket from him.

FOUR

'What's wrong?' Brian asked.

'This.' Helen was reading a letter. 'It's from Amman.'

General bright talk for a page and a half about his first impressions of the Middle East, then: 'I said nothing on the phone before I left because I didn't want to worry you, but on the Saturday night I was a hair's breadth away from swallowing a whole bottle of valium. I desperately needed to phone you at two a.m., but was scared of waking Brian. Thank God for Jason, who turned up unexpectedly. (He saw the lights on as he was driving past, and stopped to tell me of his mother's death. He'd been out to dinner with friends in Stoke Newington, and was looking for a last drink before he went home.) He talked me through till breakfast-time. . . The reasons for the suddenness of the depression were solely to do with that hateful hour at the Phoenix: hiding my real feelings from Donald was in retrospect a deplorable self-degradation, a *total* loss this time of self-respect.

'I can't begin to describe it, Saturday night: the real horrors. Not the rush of blood, the butterflies of sexual jealousy; but something almost external that seized me as if I was in a vice. I just *knew* that in ten minutes, or half an hour maybe, I would pick up those pills and swallow every one of them, wash them down with quantities of whisky, and that nothing and no one could stop me. I was physically paralysed – no, I can't find words for it. I've felt the same sensation here, once, but it was not so serious, a pale echo of that Saturday – I found I was in a shop looking at poisons and trying to decide which was the least painful. I know I shouldn't tell you these things because you'll be very upset (I can see you now and hear what you're saying to Brian) but the moment I start concealing anything from you there's something wrong with our relationship. It isn't pining for Donald; it's more a knowledge of waste that hits me – yes, self-pity I know but it's no good suppressing it; I have to get it up and out of the system, recognizing it for what it is. Maybe if I slept with a beautiful man here I'd feel differently, but I can't deal at the moment with sex, not in any way. It would just leave me with an even greater sense of futility. As for Donald, I feel I ought to be purged of him now instead of wanting him for what he is (or, rather, was); it's like a virus, my love for him, and has to be killed.

'I'm sorry. I wish I could spare you this; it's not fucking nice of me. Saying it – well – perhaps it helps the attempt to get rid of it. I don't think it's an inevitable downward spiral, but it's the sheer pointlessness of existence after Donald that just hurts too much. I ought to be writing this to him, not to you. Why should I distress you, and spare him? O.K., I know he's your little brother. You and I once talked about falling out of love; I remember you saying that no one could be blamed for it. Quite true, quite right. But if he stopped loving me, why couldn't he say so and leave me alone? And if not – well, what, why? What meaning has it, what explanation? I wake every morning with the need to adjust because sleep makes me forget – oh, he's not here beside me. It's always the worst moment of the day. I feel morally unclean – as if he has raped or defiled (I don't know what the right word is) what was between us: maybe it never was worth having – a dolls' house.

'A few weeks ago we went to the cinema. He said, "I love you tonight because we're here and it's *Cabaret* and the ambiance is so good." Yuck. Shallow as a drying pool. Am I beginning to hate him? That's only a kind of loving. I long to feel total indifference. I'm sleepy now, valium-sleepy: another day has passed. I'm living in a sort of men-o-pause. Goodnight.'

Brian was silent for some time, then said, 'I've nothing to say. Even if I felt all that, which I have done, I couldn't write such a letter. My own marriage breaking up. I wouldn't talk to someone in that way.'

'You're a very different person.'

'Yes. This constant verbalising, this pouring himself like so much golden syrup over other people, you . . . I don't understand it. Perhaps I just disapprove. What was all that about the Phoenix?'

'It was their anniversary –'

'No. Don't tell me! I don't want to know.' He looked again at the letter, then said, 'You certainly do have a close relationship with him.'

'What do you mean?'

'All this fag-hag stuff. I don't understand it. I feel left out, I suppose.'

'Left out? Are you telling me you're . . . jealous?'

'Am I?'

'Shit!' She stood up and walked round the room, then came back to the breakfast table. 'Would you like some more coffee?'

Brian laughed. 'What an extraordinary thing to say! In the circumstances. Only *you* would say that.'

Helen ran her fingers through her hair. 'What you said . . . it bothers me. I didn't realise.'

'Don't take it more seriously than it was meant. I was talking without thinking first . . . as Mark would. Really, it isn't important.' They looked at each other, both somewhat surprised. 'It is *not* important,' he said again.

'What was your reaction to it all?' Ted asked. They were sitting in their garden; Jason, who had not been to bed all night, was still dressed in his motor-bike leathers, dark glasses and helmet.

'I felt very, very sorry for him.' He ground out his cigarette. 'I thought I should stay there . . . I'm sorry I had to wake you at two thirty in the morning, but if I hadn't phoned to tell you where I was, Christ knows what you would have imagined . . . dead under a lorry or something. We talked till seven a.m. Or rather, *he* did. People in that state . . . they say some very weird things.'

114

'What things?'

'I don't want to repeat them.' He looked up, stretched, and yawned. 'I tried to persuade him to let me share his bed. But he wouldn't.'

'What good would that have done?'

'I don't mean I wanted to have sex with him! God . . . no! I thought someone ought to hold him, kiss him, be tender with him. I wanted to do that.'

'Hmm.'

Jason grinned. 'You're jealous! Well . . . my memory might be playing tricks, but I seem to recall that he looks very nice stark naked.' He gestured, obscenely. '*And* . . . so I'm told . . . he's rather efficient at it.'

Ted laughed. 'Everyone's efficient in bed with the right man. Or inefficient with the wrong man.'

'The point is I didn't . . . and don't . . . want to have sex with him. Only with you. You're quite well aware of that. But . . . what a mess! Fancy letting someone push you so far! Their relationship should have broken up years back. Mark thinks they were the envy of the gay world, but I never envied them. Sticking together because of the shared furniture, and Donald not enjoying sex unless it was with someone else!' He shook his head. 'Ridiculous!'

'Hundreds of gay couples have lived like that. Do so even now, despite AIDS.'

'Well, it wouldn't suit me. There's one thing about us Donald and Mark haven't had for years: I can't get enough of your body. It astonishes me, but . . . I can't.'

'It's that important?'

'For Christ's sake, yes! Good sex, fabulous sex: what's the point of having a lover without that?'

'For some people having a lover is . . . status. Security. A position in society.'

Jason snorted. 'The best position for a lover is underneath me on a mattress!' He finished his coffee. 'Or the other way round. Something else about Mark I don't accept is this running to straight friends like Helen with all his problems. Why doesn't he talk to you?'

115

'He did on one occasion.'

'He knows you'd say it's finished. I guess he doesn't want to face that truth.' He yawned again. 'I don't think I care for Donald all that much.'

'Why?'

'Too needy. Too greedy.' He stood up and went indoors. 'I can hardly move, I'm so tired! Good thing it's Sunday. Will you cook my breakfast?'

Ted followed him into the kitchen, and began to beat up some eggs. 'Too needy, too greedy,' he said. 'My first lover was a bit like that. A student, a nineteen-year-old, and I'd just started teaching; I was twenty-three. Well, we were together five years –'

'That's long, for a first relationship.'

Ted laughed. 'Look who's talking! Anyway . . . when he was at university I didn't charge him rent, or ask for a share of the electricity or the gas or the rates or the phone bill –'

Jason poured himself another coffee. 'You were crazy!'

'He wasn't mean with his money, what little he had. So I didn't mind, though I'd say it was a relationship of unequal dependences, and that, eventually, spells trouble. What really annoyed me was after he graduated: he made no serious effort to look for a job. I nagged, but it was useless. Then I went off to Canada for two months and left him behind. I wasn't going to subsidise his holidays too. When I came back he'd got himself a job all right. In Leeds. So he fucked off, and that was the last I heard of him. He never had any intention of finding work near where we lived, never was going to stop so long that he'd have to pay for something! I was tricked all the way along the line! I'll not forgive him for that.'

'It still hurts?'

'Yes. We all get hurt at least once in a lifetime. I said it was a relationship of unequal dependences. Well . . . *I* was the dependent one. I only found that out afterwards.'

'Like Mark.'

Ted nodded. 'Like Mark.'

116

'But you weren't tempted to try the valium and whisky cure?'

'No. No . . . I just whored around. I had a fling with Malcolm, and all I can say about him is that he fucked like a donkey.' Jason raised an eyebrow. Ted smiled, then said, 'That's not the whole truth . . . there were other things. So I got hurt once more, but not so much. You develop . . . a kind of immunity. Then I met Alan.'

'Security inside yourself.'

'But you lose something on the way.'

Jason tucked into the scrambled eggs. 'Yes. Well . . . when I've eaten this, we can go upstairs and discover how far off break-up *we* are.'

'I thought you said you were so weary you could hardly move.'

'I just want your arms round me in bed so I can fall asleep like that.' He began to sing, *You're the one that I want*. 'Let's go to Benjy's tonight.'

'Don't you ever get tired of dancing?'

'No.'

'Nor do I,' Ted admitted. 'Not since I discovered how good it can be. And that's thanks to you.'

'Your letter was very welcome,' Helen wrote, 'though as you guessed it disturbed me greatly. Where do I start? A whole crowd of points in my head jostle for attention and make me feel it's impossible to focus them – whatever I say in a few lines is bound to be trite. It isn't necessary to enumerate the reasons why it's not worth desperation. What happened to you sounds like a state of mind, induced logically *and* illogically from the previous events, in which all other issues are clouded and the feeling of self-disgust is mirrored by the sense of failure, rejection, and futility. Your own value, in your eyes and those of others, seemed at that time to be lessened. This inflicts a sense of hurt deeper even than that caused by rejection and the loss of secure love, and then one faces the question: not – can I go on? Clearly one can. But – to what end? I don't propose to list the choices – you are well aware of the answers. I'm convinced you *will* find a balance

117

and that you have the potential to achieve real happiness again. As far as I'm concerned, there are obvious limits to the amount I can help you. I fear the support system must be insufficient if you need a safety net at two a.m. You were probably right not to phone – Brian would not have been all that sympathetic – but I'm sorry not to have been able to assist at a nadir point. However, you know that the will to help is not switched off – it's there the whole time, and I can only hope the knowledge of that may contribute towards getting you through the bad periods. I've told you you're not accountable to me. The only thing that would make me think less of you is your looking favourably on that bottle of pills, or anything comparable.

'Your descriptions of Amman interested me, and I laughed at the "men-o-pause" . . . Donald was here yesterday and we spent an hour chatting about nothing in particular, our parents, a bit about you, though there wasn't much to say that hadn't been said before. Determination not to be committed, not to have any binding relationships, not to face questions like "When will I see you again?" His attitude is that if you and he *are* to see each other, it might as well be made as pleasant and unstressful as possible. I'm sure I'm not telling you anything you don't know already. It was a fairly superficial chat; he seemed quite well and relatively cheerful, though not wildly happy or energetic. Is he ever these days? He knows my views, and will shrug his metaphorical shoulders and do something else.

'All is well here, despite Angela falling into a blackberry bush. Really, that child is so clumsy! Why didn't my husband bequeathe her some of his agility? Brian has been busy in the garden and is becoming increasingly peppery with colleagues at work, though we had a pleasant weekend (weather not bad for once this foul summer) – Saturday at Greenwich and Sunday with my parents.'

Brian wrote more tersely. 'It appears that you are splenetic: I do sympathise for I feel you have some cause. But it's most unprofitable and fearfully bad for the digestion. Seriously: I have no solution, for, as we both know, you and I are wholly opposite in temperament. I

118

too have experienced sad sour times, and I found that all one achieves – or suffers – or realises – is an erosion.

'One is diminished. The exercise of anger reduces the capacity for affection or love. It is not extravagant to see in any man a whole measure which he may decant as he pleases into bile or choler, or into another human being. You hardly want nor need a lecture from me, but, to be quite plain, the object of your affections isn't worth the effort. He really is *not*! By all means smash an entire dinner service – the satisfaction is momentary – and the replacement cost excessive. Or join the Foreign Legion, or the Trappists, but fretting at an unhealed wound. . .

'I'm going back to my tomatoes. Helen is still writing. It must be emphatic stuff – the table wobbles, biro-stabbed.'

I've known Mark for seventeen years, he said to himself, and this is the first time I've written him a letter.

Helen said, 'Mark thinks the only predictable aspect of Donald's behaviour is that it's consistently and totally unpredictable. I wouldn't agree with him. My brother is becoming banal.'

'Yes,' Brian answered. 'I wouldn't live with that sort of nonsense.'

'We know most of the layers of our particular onion, I guess. The sharing, the nights in, the nights out, the jokes no one else understands . . . being conscious of what we each think before we're even thinking it. Nothing inscrutable about *us*.'

'Nothing?'

'Except perhaps the absolute centre of you. You showed me some of that the other day.'

'Ah. My inability to understand the faggery-haggery.'

'Yes.'

'I don't want to discuss that.'

'Why not?'

'Helen! Don't provoke me!'

Helen, shopping further afield than usual, found herself in Tottenham. Donald was outside the place where their mother worked, loading some boxes into the Fiat. She paused; the last thing she wanted at that moment was a conversation with her brother. She decided to avoid him by going into the church nearby; maybe there was a door on the other side of it through which she could slip out. Last night, in bed, she and Brian had experienced something that was almost like a serious quarrel. It seemed to reveal a part of his character she did not approve of, the existence of which she hadn't noticed since they were teenagers.

One of the greatest joys of this second relationship with Brian – so she thought – was their sensitivity to each other. Unlike when they were at school, they were aware of shifts of mood almost before such changes happened; there was, she considered, a complete naturalness about the way their giving and taking slotted together. Yet last night he had been extraordinarily insensitive. There was no doubt that he was jealous of her friendship with Mark. Not, of course, sexually; he wasn't so stupid as to think a gay man posed any threat of that kind: it was a realisation that Mark had qualities he had not, that touched something in her which he could not satisfy.

'Talking about it,' she said, 'means you aren't keeping it to yourself; you're telling me, the sympathetic listener.'

'And I wish I wasn't!' Brian answered.

'Why?'

'I don't know.'

She thought for a moment. 'Neither do I,' she admitted.

'Well . . . that's bad.'

'Is it really important?'

'Oh yes, Helen, it is!'

'What do you want me to do? Not see Mark? Forbid him to come to the house?'

'Don't be ridiculous!'

'Well . . . what?'

'I don't want you to do anything in particular.'

'I've known Mark as long as I've known you,' she said. 'But when I was at university, and for a couple of years after, I didn't know you at all. I went on seeing Mark of course . . . he was my brother's lover, for God's sake! So there's a whole pattern of shared experiences in which

120

you didn't participate . . . parties, trips to the theatre, old friends, and so on. Yes, Mark and I do need each other; I miss him if weeks go by without even a phone call. It's not painful, missing him – it's not like *you* being away. But he's in the fabric of my existence. I can't alter that.'

'It's incomprehensible to me! You, the children, my house, my garden: that's my private world. I don't like anybody else being part of it. Oh, I don't mean I'm anti-social, that I hate seeing friends, but . . . sometimes I feel I'm sharing my wife with another man.'

This last remark shocked her. 'I'm sorry,' she said. 'But I don't know what to do about it. The letter I wrote to Mark . . . I showed it to you. I stressed that my sympathies, my ability to help, had clear limitations.'

'Did you? I got the opposite impression.'

'Brian! Really!'

'Yes. Really.' He turned over, pulling the quilt round himself, and switched off the light. She lay awake for a long time. It was a fuss about nothing in her opinion, a mirage in Brian's head. And this bothered her. She had never seen him before as someone likely to be a prey to fantasies; he always had such a firm grip on real, practical things. That intuitiveness they shared; it was not so perfect after all. How well did she know him? He had lived with, then married, a woman she knew almost nothing about. And the years from nineteen to twenty-four were, in anybody's life, rich with experience; no wonder she caught Mark's eye or glanced at Donald when a reference was made to some detail from the past which only they knew. Why couldn't Brian understand and accept?

The church, the summer sun streaming through its windows, was a mass of subtle lights and shadows. The warmth of its stone! She listened to its whispers, absorbed its peace.

Then she almost literally bumped into her father, who was coming out of the vestry. 'Hullo, hullo, hullo!' he boomed, shattering a century of calm. 'What are you doing here?'

'Just passing through.'

121

'I'm arranging a deal with the vicar. He's going to flog me the lead from the roof!' His laugh echoed round the vault.

'How's Donald?' She remembered words from a prayer: beware of loud and aggressive persons for they are vexatious to the spirit.

'Moving to Liverpool. Miles away! He's actually got a job at last, in independent radio. Standing on his own two feet for once, thank God. Even for small mercies. I don't know how Mark's taking it.'

And you're not particularly worried, Helen thought. 'He's in Jordan,' she said. 'I had a postcard yesterday from Ma'an.'

'Jordan! Well, it's all right for some. Can't stop, Helen. I'm meeting a friend for lunch.' He winked. 'A liquid lunch.'

She left him and went outside. A tree in bloom, sunlight, lilac, stone. I must talk to Brian, she said to herself.

FIVE

Jordan did not heal his wounds, but it was at least a novel and exciting experience. He left England on the last day of July and returned at the end of August, fit and well, his inward eye full of landscapes more spectacular, savage and barren than anything he had ever seen or imagined. Nor did the men-o-pause last long. He went to bed with a young Australian he met in Amman: 'He turned me on fantastically,' he said later to Helen, deliberately echoing Donald's words about Rick.

The Australian took him to the Dead Sea, which was so saline he found he could sit on it. They drove to Aqaba, and stopped by the rock Moses struck to bring water to the desert: Mark struck it too – it was a logan-stone balanced on the top of an artesian well – and water trickled. By the Hejaz railway he saw a rusting train lying on its side; it had been blown up by T.E. Lawrence and his companions in the First World War. Nobody, in over half a century, had bothered to remove it. At Petra, the extraordinary beauty of the houses and the palaces, carved out of the mountains long before the birth of Christ, moved him to tears. He watched an elderly Arab woman digging in the sand: she found an ancient Nabataean pot, and he bought it from her. It was nearly three thousand years old. He and the Australian ate couscous that night with some wandering Arabs, and slept together in the open air on the sand, outside one of Petra's temples. This is as far from the existence I've lived, he said to himself, as I've ever been. Dressed only in shorts, his skin the colour of mahogany, hair bleached white by the sun, he was almost unrecognizable. And elated. For the first time in ten years a day could pass when he did not think of Donald.

So, back in Amman, he was astonished, almost shocked, to find Donald had written to him. Helen, agreeing for once to be a post office, had mailed the letter. 'I love you. I love you and want you back. I'll give you a second honeymoon, a horn of plenty. I promise.' An insurance policy, he said to himself, the result of defeat; 'I promise' Donald could say as easily as 'Pass the marmalade.'

At home in a cool, green, wet September, he looked for Donald at his lodgings, but he had gone without leaving a forwarding address. Ringing Jane told him why. 'He's got a job in Liverpool,' she said. 'Something to do with the local radio station. Yes, it was on the spur of the moment . . . but I must say Chris and I are very happy about it. Two years with no work! Perhaps he'll settle down a bit now.'

'When did he leave?'

'Oh . . . a fortnight ago.'

'Can I phone him? Do you have his address?'

'I'm not sure where he's living; he didn't even know himself when he went.'

'Do you have his work number?'

'Yes.' There was a long pause, then she said, 'Mark . . . he asked me, only yesterday, not to give it to you.'

How to cope with a grief? In much the same ways as anybody else, he supposed, and he remembered the time when he thought a death would have been easier, not because of the sympathy he might receive, but because he'd know Donald was not in bed with a lover. It was not so appalling now: he'd got used to the process. These months of break-up had left him drained; never again would he have to face the raw, bleeding emotions of loss so unprepared and vulnerable. He slept at nights. He went out looking for sex – something he'd never had to do before. It was often a waste of time and money, he thought; hanging around in discos and bars buying drinks. And a condom *did* take the edge off the pleasure. But nothing was as bad as when Donald was there unable to decide whether to go or to stay. The red Fiat was not outside Rick's flat, and they could not accidentally meet in the pubs and clubs. Donald, absent, could no longer be agent provocateur to goad him to a violence that could find no outlet, ultimately, except by turning it against himself. He could at least exist.

'Our days of sunshine and happiness,' Donald had said in a letter the Christmas after they first met, 'when every day will be summer for us, together all day and every day, they seem so far in the future it frightens me. I AM SELFISH. I want you NOW, for ever, to rule over, to be mine alone, to keep safe by me, never to let go, to make you happier than you've ever been. If I should lose you I think I should die, possibly by my own hand.

'I love you, my love, so very much. I love you, I love you.'
He did not, on any single occasion, Mark said to himself, make me happier than I'd ever been. I've been happier eating good meals with Helen. Did he, at any time, really love me?

He did not, Mark decided, despite those words. True, he thought he meant what he said. But they were the words of a hysteric, and they rang false – 'If I should lose you I think I should die, possibly by my own hand.' In another letter Donald had written, 'All the time now I'm thinking about cottages in the country with dogs, a garden, roses, and naturally and primarily, you.' Sweet dreams. Paper roses. Despite the naturally and the primarily, the 'you' was an afterthought. Donald only loved him for what he had to offer. But I'm rewriting history, he told himself; it's the only way I can come to terms with it.

'All he's worried about now,' Jason said, 'is whether you're taking care of what bits of furniture belong to him, and whether – if you should meet him by accident – you'll be polite.'

'Did he want to know how I was? What I'm doing? Ask if I had a new lover? Anything?'

'No.'

Christmas morning; Jason was doing the rounds of his friends north of the river, a drink with each. He and Ted were having guests to dinner in the afternoon. Mark was going to his parents and was not looking forward to it; Christmas in Croydon was not an exciting prospect. 'I'm a person,' he said, 'who hopes my lover will behave in the same way as I do. No . . . not just hopes, I *assume* he does. Obviously that's a mistake. I shall have to learn to be more suspicious.'

'It's a mistake – if that's the right word, and I'm not sure that it is – which everybody makes.'

'Everybody?'

'Some, then.'

'I assume he has a similar moral code, a similar view of responsibilities.'

'You think if you were Donald you'd have behaved differently?'

'Of course!'

'You wouldn't have been so indecisive,' Jason conceded. 'Nor so selfish. But the hurt would be just as big. And . . . don't think Donald is without problems adjusting.'

'What problems?'

'I didn't discuss that with him. But not even he can chuck out a whole decade and have no regrets.' He glanced at his watch. 'I must go. I can't trust Ted to look after that goose for too long! I won't say have a marvellous Christmas because I'm sure you will not . . . but get through it as best you can.'

'I'll try.'

'Mark . . . may I suggest we have a moratorium on the subject of Donald?'

'You're bored.'

'It's not that. Chewing it all over so relentlessly . . . it does no good.'

'Did Ted invite Donald to dinner?'

'Leave it, Mark! No, Ted didn't invite him to dinner. I met Donald yesterday for what he chooses to call a casual drink. When he phoned he was fishing madly for an invitation, but we really couldn't be bothered. Besides,

126

Ted guessed what was happening and waved his arms around like a windmill, then he wrote on a piece of paper "NO!" '

'I think you disapprove of what Donald's done,' Mark said.

'Why do you want to know? Would it make you feel better?'

'Yes.'

Jason laughed. 'You don't need me or Ted to spell out which of you we prefer!' He looked at his watch again. 'The goose! I'm going . . . goodbye, Mark.'

One Sunday morning two weeks later Mark was lying on the settee reading a novel. Silence within and without, though if he listened hard enough he could hear people walking along the towpath. He was looking forward to the rest of the day; he was going, at lunch-time, to a party in Stockwell. Richard's parties were always excellent: plenty of wine and good food, and the proceedings often continued all afternoon, sometimes far into the night.

There was a knock on the door. Bloody Jehovah's Witnesses, he thought as he went to answer it; they were the only people who called on a Sunday morning. It was Jane. With her, a big, hairy man he'd never seen before, looming like a macho bodyguard. 'A neighbour of ours,' she said, introducing him. 'This is off my own bat. . .' She was trying to sound calm, but was evidently concealing some considerable agitation. 'I want to say at once that Donald knows nothing about it. I've come to collect his furniture. I know that having it here causes you a lot of distress. It will be much better for all of us if I take his things away now, and that will be that. We've . . . hired a truck.'

A carefully rehearsed speech; that was obvious. 'Distress?' Mark was bewildered. 'It isn't causing me any distress. What are you talking about?'

'May we come in?'

He thought for a moment, then said, 'I suppose so.'

A mistake: once inside, her nervous manner disappeared and she became cool and business-like; gaining

127

an entry was the only difficulty she had foreseen. 'I've a list here,' she said. 'That chair, Ian' – to the bodyguard – 'take that out to start with. Then the dining-room table.'

'Wait a minute,' Mark said. 'Just wait a minute! You can't come bursting in and walk off with half the contents of my flat!'

'Only the half that belongs to my son.'

'But . . . I use it! What am I going to do for a dining-table? Donald *must* have put you up to this!'

'No, he did not.'

'You're a liar! You're all liars, the whole lot of you!'

She ignored that and said, in the patient tone of voice a nurse might use with a raving lunatic, 'There's no need to upset yourself. What I'm doing is best for all of us; and Donald has *not*, I repeat, put me up to this. As a matter of fact, he hasn't even told me why he left you.'

'Lies. Lies!'

'It's the truth. I can only assume that you made his life so impossible he had to get out.'

'That is an extraordinary thing to say!'

'Extraordinary or not, he's gone, and I'm looking after his interests.'

Ian, great gorilla, picked up the table as if it was a toy and carried it out to the truck. 'Bookcase next?' he asked. He began to remove the books from the top shelf.

'You leave them alone!' Mark shouted. 'Those are mine, and the bookcase belongs to Donald *and* me!'

'No, it doesn't,' Jane said.

It had belonged to her. It was the one she and Chris were going to chop up for firewood.

'You gave it to us,' Mark said.

'I did not. I lent it to you.'

'That is not what Donald told me!'

'I'm sure he told you the truth. Take the books out, Ian.'

Mark picked up the phone. 'If you touch it, I'll call the police!'

Ian paused.

'All right, leave it,' Jane said. 'We'll sort that out some other time.' Mark put the receiver down. After he had done so, she said to Ian, 'The television.'

128

Mark was rapidly losing his temper. 'Don't you dare touch it!' he yelled. 'Get out, both of you. GET OUT!!'

Ian raised himself to his full height and clenched his fists. 'Now then,' Jane said. 'None of that! I don't want any trouble.'

'I'm sure you don't,' Mark said. 'You'd end up in court, wouldn't you! Then you'd look rather stupid!'

The bodyguard was undoubtedly aching to squash Mark into pulp. Fucking fairies, he was probably thinking; deserve all they get. Should be wiped off the map.

'We'd better go,' Jane said. She had obviously not worked out what she should do in the eventuality of Mark resisting. Ian's presence, she might have decided, would be enough to cower him into acquiescence. Strange that Chris had not accompanied her, Mark thought. I-wash-my-hands-of-it-all.   It's-nothing-to-do-with-me.   Shame-that-gay-relationships-are-so-unstable.   Always-end-in-tears.

'We'll be back,' Ian said, as he and Jane went to the door. 'Don't you think for one minute that we won't!'

'I didn't want it to turn out like this,' Jane said.

'You should have thought more carefully,' Mark answered. 'But you probably aren't capable of that.'

He slammed the door behind them as hard as he could. He found he was trembling. Why is it, he said to himself, that the only person he'd met in his whole life who made him so violent and destructive was Donald? He paced round the flat looking for something of Donald's to smash into tiny pieces: it would at least relieve his feelings. Wouldn't it? No. It wouldn't.

He poured himself a large glass of sherry and swallowed it in one mouthful. And another. Then he drove across the river to Stockwell, to Richard's party, where by late afternoon he had drunk himself unconscious.

'It all seems rather strange,' Helen said. 'Very out of character.' They were in the house at East Finchley.

'Yes, it is,' Mark replied. 'I don't understand it.'

'People sometimes get a fixed idea in their heads, and they can't consider anything else till they've done what

129

they set out to do. Maybe that was it. Though I wonder what Donald's contribution was to the whole fiasco.'

'She stressed he had no part in it.'

Helen frowned. 'Do you believe that?'

'Of course not. They're all liars. I'm sorry, Helen . . . I shouldn't be talking like this about your family.'

'Her behaviour was certainly . . . not within the normal bounds of civilised intercourse.'

He laughed. 'I do like your discreet English! "Not within the normal bounds of civilised intercourse!" I don't know. I don't know how much more I can take.'

'You'll survive.'

'You overestimate me. You always do.'

'You underestimate yourself.'

'You're marvellous, Helen! I wish you were a man! With green eyes and high cheek-bones –'

'And long dark hair. Male footballer's body. Donald.'

'Yes.' They both laughed.

'If you were a man I'd steal you from Brian.'

'Don't say things like that!'

He looked at her, surprised; the expression on her face was serious. 'I'm . . . sorry. I was only joking. . . Is something wrong?'

Brian came into the room. 'The meal is ready,' he said. 'Probably overcooked. Angela's sitting at the table and I'm sure that wretched toddler of ours will come in from next door any minute now. Look. There he is! I have second sight.'

Helen finished her drink.

'I'd better go,' Mark said. Neither of them pressed him to stay.

Donald, at work one morning, felt unwell, as if he had a hangover. Odd, he thought; he hadn't been drinking the previous night. By the end of the day he was feverish; light-headed almost. He was shocked when he took his temperature that evening – a hundred and four. He went to bed, but did not sleep well; he dozed, and woke from nightmarish dreams, then dozed again. Next morning, feeling slightly better, he dragged himself to the doctor's:

nothing much anyone could prescribe for what was clearly a nasty bout of flu, but at least he might be able to get something to push his temperature down. The doctor took his time with the examination. He's being strangely thorough, Donald said to himself; they're usually writing the prescription before you've finished telling them the symptoms. 'You're going to the nearest hospital,' the doctor said. 'At once. It's pneumonia.'

The next week was a blank; it might as well not have existed for all Donald could remember of it – a few fleeting images of tubes, nurses, blood tests, masks, gloves. After eight days he was better, and was told, very gently and compassionately, that he had had pneumocystis carinii, that his immune system was severely impaired: that he had AIDS. His first reaction was that it couldn't be true; he had not once since the beginning of the break-up with Mark swallowed sperm or been screwed without a condom. But, the counsellor said, he could have been carrying the virus for years. There had been times, even as long ago as when they were at Sussex, that Donald, in Mark's absence, had slept with other men and not given a moment's thought to condoms. In the late seventies and early eighties nobody did. It had seemed to him a healthy pastime: it proved that no one was more right for him than Mark, however expert the other body; the hunt was always enjoyable, and scoring showed he was still attractive – it made him feel good about himself. He never told Mark of these adventures, for Mark didn't indulge in that kind of thing. Donald considered him foolish for not doing so – what on earth harm could it possibly lead to? It might make him feel good about himself.

But it had, perhaps, led to AIDS.

In a panic he phoned Mark. There was no reply. Mark was away all weekend; a month previously he had met a man who was quickly becoming his new lover, and Donald, that Saturday and Sunday, was further from his mind than he'd ever been. Saying to himself that how you cope with a grief is to love another person was the only moment he thought of Donald. He was in the new man's bed most of the weekend.

Donald phoned Helen.

'I said he could stay for as long as he wanted. Brian . . . Brian, talk to me!'

He hugged her, kissed her. 'I'm . . . beyond words. I can't have an instant reaction to something like this.'

'He says that on no account should Mum and Dad be told. On no account!'

'Then you must keep it to yourself.'

'He wanted to know if Mark is away . . . no reply, apparently, when he phoned. I said I had no idea; I haven't seen Mark for ages. According to Ted, he has a new lover, so he's probably with him. Brian . . . I think Mark should be kept out of this. Donald has caused him enough suffering. Let him enjoy his life for a bit.'

'He's bound to answer his phone sooner or later.'

'I said to Donald that my one condition for not breathing a word to Mum and Dad is that he doesn't tell Mark. I . . . mmm . . . mentioned the new lover. Was that . . . cruel?'

'No.'

She ran her fingers through her hair several times, and said, 'I can't take it in!'

After a long silence, Brian said, as gently as he could, 'Is it wise to have Donald here? Is it safe?'

'What do you mean, safe?'

'O.K. . . . we know what the experts say about this disease . . . it's caught through blood and sperm and so on; it's impossible to get it from casual contacts . . . but . . . can we be sure? I suppose there's no need to worry about crockery and cutlery, the glass he drinks from, so long as we do the washing-up properly . . . but I know I'll be wiping the lavatory seat before I sit on it –'

'Brian!'

'And the children? He's their uncle. Do we allow them to kiss him? Helen, we can't. But how do we stop them? And if he, for some reason or other, has to manage when they cut themselves, graze their legs. . .'

'Christ!' Helen sat bolt upright. 'I hadn't thought of that!' She looked at him in dismay, and said, 'What the fuck are we going to do?'

132

It was a problem they didn't have to face. The day before Donald was due to arrive, a second bout of pneumocystis carinii put him in hospital again. A week later he was dead.

Mark was with him, holding his hand. He'd been at the bedside for twelve hours – Helen had phoned him when the hospital authorities told her that Donald might not survive. He drove her up to Liverpool immediately. It was only when they were halfway there that she realised she should, on this occasion, have rung her parents. Jane and Chris, when Brian broke the news to them of Donald's death, were unaware that he had been ill.

The shock to them was, of course, appalling; and their fury with Helen – brief though it was – was understandable. They never knew their son had had AIDS. Dad in particular, Helen thought, would not be able to deal with it; he'd drink himself into his coffin. Donald, as far as they were concerned, died of pneumonia. Though mostly it didn't, it could happen to anyone; it had no stigma. But Jane thought it might have been AIDS. When she asked – Helen, Brian, Mark – for their opinion, they assured her it was not.

Donald, during the twelve hours Mark was with him, was unconscious most of the time. There were a few moments, however, when he recognized who it was by his bed, and he gripped Mark's hand tightly. He said, 'I've always loved you. If I said anything else it was a lie.' Later, restless and feverish, he asked if Ted had scrubbed the paint off. He slept, then woke to say, 'They're huge. Like plums.' He smiled. 'I'll never taste them again. I hope . . . what is his name? . . . appreciates them too.'

'He does.'

'What *is* his name?'

'Colin.'

Half an hour passed. Then a final gripping of Mark's hand, and his breathing stopped.

Mark knew there should be a whole variety of emotions he ought to be feeling – knew that in the weeks and months to come he *would* feel them – but for some days he experienced only guilt: because his reaction was a sense of relief. He had often thought, and said, during the break-up, that he'd have coped better if Donald was dead, not in another place with somebody else. It was as if a wish had come true. The virus, the succubus, Donald had become no longer existed. I can, Mark said to himself, begin with a clean slate. As if I'm reborn. Or I will be, if my AIDS test is negative.

He made love with Colin three, four, five times a night; roughly, even violently, as if to reassure himself that he was alive, a sentient, living, breathing creature death couldn't touch. The moments of orgasm were a sneer at death; losing himself in the most pleasurable of all sensations was a victory for life: Death, where is thy sting, Grave thy victory?

'I understand,' Colin said when Mark explained and apologised. 'I feel it too.'

'Tomorrow I get the result of the test. Perhaps we'll have something to celebrate. It would be nice not to have to bother with these again.' He threw the condom he'd just used onto the floor.

The night after the funeral, Jason, lying against Ted, sobbed for a while. 'He didn't deserve it,' he said. 'He did not deserve it!'

Ted stroked him, kissed him. 'Helen and Brian are doing this too, I imagine. And Mark and his Colin. Each couple, warm and tight in their burrows, reassuring one another that they still exist.'

'And Donald's parents?'

'Ah. That I don't know.'

'He was never so awful as Mark seemed to think. He just fell out of love. Nothing reprehensible in that.'

'At which point he began to behave badly,' Ted said. 'He wasn't prepared to let go of what he had till he found a better alternative; then he took so long making decisions he caused a great deal of unnecessary suffering.'

'The sheer chance of things . . . us . . . that I've never wanted anyone else . . . never been to bed with anyone else –'

'That's not true!'

'It is! Wanking with another boy at school doesn't count.'

'On one occasion during a lesson of mine! If I'd have known what was going on, I'd have. . .'

'Yes? What?'

Ted laughed. 'I don't know. It's a situation, in twenty-six years of teaching, I've never had to deal with.'

'Well, you did get boring with *The Nun's Priest's Tale*. I just happened to notice Mark had a whopping erection . . . which gave me one. I was actually coming when you asked me to translate! We didn't say a word to each other – just did it. So he never knew then that I was gay . . . I didn't really know myself. I should have done; I was already in love with you, but I wouldn't admit it. We did it a second time in one of the school bogs. Took all our clothes off.'

'Not very aesthetic, mutual masturbation in a toilet.'

'No,' Jason agreed. 'It was before he and Donald started . . . I wish I'd come out to them during all that graffiti business. But, as I said, I didn't know I was, and even if I had known, I'd have been too frightened.'

'Of other people doing to you what they were doing to Donald?'

'Yes. What went wrong between Helen and Mark? Big butch Brian didn't like her being a fag-hag and put his foot down?'

'Not really that. He felt she was paying too much attention to somebody else.'

'Male chauvinist louse!'

'She thought of Mark as her brother-in-law,' Ted said. 'Family.'

'Now the link that joined them's gone. The sheer, horrible, fucking chance of it!'

'I'll never forget when they came here for a drink. That first time: the look on Donald's face. So much in love.'

135

'I once told Mark, the night he nearly killed himself, that he ought to sell his flat. He was going on about it being a Donald museum. Or did he say mausoleum? "An everlasting reminder of the perfection and imperfection of what was," he said.'

'I suppose . . . . that's . . . a good epitaph for Donald.'

'Make love to me.' Jason's voice was urgent. 'I'm frightened.'

'Of what?'

'Death. Life. Crossing the road. Having been born.'

'Frightened of me?'

'No. Never. Never.' He shifted and wriggled until Ted was lying on top of him. 'I want you inside me. Prove that we both still exist!'

Afterwards, he began to cry again. He sobbed himself asleep, Ted's protecting arms round him.